STAR STORIES

BEGINNINGS

AUDREY FAYE

INTRODUCTION

This is a volume of short stories, companion tales that fit in The Fixers of KarmaCorp series. They started off as add-ons, but Raven now insists that they are part of the required reading. You'll need them to fully enjoy her book.

These stories are meant to fill in some of the small, interesting nooks and crannies in a world that has many of them. I hope they will add to the richness of the longer stories I tell, and provide you small delights as you read a snippet of history from a character you already love, or tease you to go read their longer story.

Audrey

FIND THE FOUR

THIS WAS a foolish waste of time.

Yesenia Mayes stepped into the loud, brisk, and vividly colorful market of Tezuli Spaceport and cursed the gut instinct that had dragged her a week out of her way and lightyears from common sense. Fixers didn't respond to whispers in the wind, and the anonymous comm message she'd received that had bounced through three quadrants before it landed on her tablet didn't even qualify as a whisper.

Even so, the content had chilled her soul.

She looked around, eyes and ears taking in her surroundings even if her mind was inexcusably wandering. It was midday in the spaceport's diurnal cycle, and the populace clustered around stalls and blanket displays doing brisk business suggested that the market was both busy and safe. Elders and children roamed freely, and the friendly greetings between customers and vendors indicated both familiarity and respect.

Not the kind of place that needed a Fixer, at least on the surface. And certainly not a place that sent messages to KarmaCorp's newly minted Director for the quadrant.

Yesenia shifted slightly as a small boy ran her direction, hotly pursued by three of his friends. The steaming bun in his hands suggested the reason for the chase. She gave the boy in the lead a sharp look as he ducked by her, and then relaxed. His cheeks were far too chubby to belong to a child who truly needed food.

On her home world, such a pursuit would have been in deadly earnest—and the child carrying such treasure far more skilled at hiding their bounty.

KarmaCorp's reach was vast, and the Federated Commonwealth of Planets had no tolerance for starving children, but neither of those meant it didn't happen. She knew that far better than most. There were always underbellies, corners of the universe good at making themselves hard to find. Enclaves of the lawless or the desperate.

"Mi'dama, might I help you?"

Yesenia looked down in surprise. The shopkeeper who had been brave enough to accost her came barely to her shoulder, and his wizened face showed no signs of fear.

She blinked—perhaps he was blind. No one looked at her without fear, not these days. She was Traveler Yesenia Mayes, KarmaCorp's most legendary Fixer, or at least its most terrifying one—and these days, a standard fixture on galactic vid screens. And for those who didn't recognize her on sight, the lethal look in her eyes was generally enough. "I'm not buying."

The man's face carved into a well-lined grin as he met her gaze with a direct one of his own. "I can see that well enough."

Not blind, then. She took a closer look—anonymous message senders might come in any sort of guise. Her Talent didn't pick up anything different than what her eyes had already seen. An old man, serenely confident in who he was and extending a simple offer of help.

Not something Yesenia Mayes was used to taking. "I had some time to kill between my shuttles. Someone mentioned that the market was a good place to spend a few hours."

The man who had apparently designated himself her companion chuckled. "It is that, indeed. I'm Tamsin. Perhaps you might do an old man the pleasure of letting him introduce you to the jewel of Tezuli Spaceport."

The market looked like a jewel—a boisterous and flamboyant one. Yesenia considered, and then gave him a sharp nod. A good Fixer knew the value of local contacts, and the message she had received had been long on fear-mongering and short on useful details. Perhaps an old man with wise eyes could be helpful in that regard.

Or perhaps he'd been sent. She wasn't a big believer in coincidence. Paranoia had served her very well over the years.

"Are you at all hungry, mi'dama?" Tamsin had somehow managed to herd her into a stroll down one of the larger aisles—without laying a hand on her person.

Judging from the level of casual physical contact around her, that wasn't a cultural norm. She filed that data away, not yet drawing conclusions. "I could perhaps eat a small snack." She had a terrible weakness for market food—the legacy of a child who had once thought it the pinnacle of achievement to have enough coin in her pocket to buy some.

She had never stolen, not even in the worst of hunger.

What she had done instead might have been worse.

"This way." Tamsin smiled and laid his hand on the head of a small child who waved up at him. "There are some fine food vendors just up ahead. Sweet treats and savory ones."

She chose savory, always. She could smell their teasing scents now, the tempting richness and dripping fats and mingling spices. Her taste buds gurgled out saliva in response. Yesenia kept her somewhat amused thoughts to herself. She would eat only if she determined it safe, and the hungry child inside her would just have to live with that choice.

A preteen girl stepped into their path, arms full of bright woven scarves. "Would your lady like a shawl, Tamsin?" She smiled up at Yesenia. "They're a wonder for keeping the chill of a shuttle off your shoulders."

Apparently nobody here knew enough to read a lack of welcome in a visitor's eyes. "I'm not buying, thank you."

The girl winked at Tamsin, not at all discouraged. "If she changes her mind, you know where to find me."

He smiled fondly and laid a hand on her cheek. "Indeed I do, m'alanna. Tell your sister the weaver that

I'll be desiring a new rug before winter—these old bones need to be kept warm."

"I'm almost ready to make a rug on my own. Perhaps one day I'll do fine enough work to grace your tent."

Yesenia felt her eyebrows winging up in surprise. "You live in tents?" That was highly unusual for a space station, and this one was far enough from the nearest planets that she'd assumed the market vendors would largely be residents of the spaceport.

The girl's laughter tinkled brightly over the general hubbub. "Only in our dreams, mi'dama. But we've kept the words of our ancestors alive to remind us who we are." She bowed and backed away, managing to navigate the crowd as if she had a set of eyes in the back of her head. "Good day to you both. Enjoy the market."

"She'll be off to help her mother," said Tamsin quietly. "She's a hard worker, that one, and very committed to her family."

Yesenia heard more in his voice, and the Song underneath it, than he was saying. "Is that why you'll buy her first rug when she makes it?"

He laughed. "Is such a thought so obvious on my face?"

Not on his face, no, but her Talent had never needed such obvious clues. Yesenia took another look around, with a Fixer's eye to the culture of the market. The color had more meaning now, as did the sketches a talented young artist was rendering at the side of the aisle.

Tamsin stayed at her shoulder as she stepped in for a closer look. He smiled as the artist paused in her sketching long enough to give them both a welcoming smile. "Melessa draws pictures of the gypsies of Earth, who we count as our cultural ancestors."

Yesenia looked more closely at the drawings. Vivid portraits, full of movement and life and even music, if such a thing could be put on a page. The girl used some kind of colored sticks and what looked like handmade paper. Her drawings were quick, rustic, and beautiful. "You're Wanderers, then." She'd met a few groups of the traveling people in the past, but never a stationary settlement.

"Of a sort." Tamsin nodded in approval as the artist picked out a red drawing stick. "We've decided that we can remain in one spot and let the world travel past us."

A spaceport was a pretty good place to watch the flow of humanity. And it meant she was a fool if she assumed they didn't know who and what she was. Wanderers didn't miss much. Smarter to assume that they knew and for some reason, didn't care—or at least weren't showing it. She looked at the man who had attached himself to her and made an educated guess. "Do you have any children here who might have some interest in coming to work for KarmaCorp?"

It was a reach, but not a long one. The Wanderers had more than their share of what they called gifts. Not precisely the same as Talents, but not entirely different, either—and it was a rare cohort of Fixers who didn't have one or two Wanderers in the mix.

Tamsin dipped his chin, acknowledging the shift in the conversation.

Yesenia noted that he didn't look at all surprised, and neither did Melessa. They knew who she was—and in all likelihood, knew why she was here. Frustration flared at the slow, winding game, but she didn't let a whiff of that show on her face. There would be a time when she would step in and demand that this dance move to her beat, but for now, she could let them set the pace.

She let her eyes travel back to the art in progress. The addition of the red, slashed through the skirt of the dancing gypsy, was making the entire drawing come alive under Melessa's flying hands.

Yesenia let her heart yearn for just a moment.

Melessa met her gaze, eyes twinkling. "It's the fourth of a series. If you come back in an hour, I can have them all tubed up for you for transport."

She wasn't here to buy art. "I didn't come to shop."

Tamsin chuckled beside her. "I'd be a very rich man if I had a tenth-credit for every visitor to the market who says that."

Yesenia's agile mind was already offering up justification. Spending a few credits to maintain good relations with the locals was merely smart protocol. The head of the Anthro team would enjoy the sketches, and the opportunity to study their materials and design.

She snorted, amused at herself for the second time in a quarter hour. Kechan would be on the first shuttle once she told him of the tribe of stationary Wanderers. She didn't need him as an excuse for a grown woman to buy something frivolous.

Melessa tipped her head down, not quite hiding her knowing smile.

Yesenia turned away, not saying anything. She was quite sure the drawings would be ready to go when she returned. She waited until they were a few steps away from the artist's blanket and then looked over at the man guiding her.

He dipped his chin again, wisely not commenting on her choice, and smoothly picking up the thread of their previous conversation instead. "No children with Talent, Traveler. Not at this time."

She let the sharp edge of frustration flare where he could see it this time. "I assume you have a very good reason for all the smoke and mirrors."

He smiled at a rotund shopkeeper and her stall of baked goods. "We are aware that we asked KarmaCorp's newest Director to voyage well out of her way based on very little information. We believe our reasons are good."

The smell of the food was getting to her. "Would you care to share that reason, or must I purchase goods from half the market as my price for the information?"

His laugh came all the way up from his belly. "We've never needed such enticements, mi'dama, and we won't be starting now." He looped a companionable hand through her elbow. "Come. I'll buy you a savory pastry and a mug of good, sweet cider, and once you've had your fill I'll take you to see Alara."

Yesenia considered planting her feet and refusing to be herded, but decided it would only make her look and feel like a recalcitrant child. "And who, pray tell, is Alara?"

When he looked at her this time, his eyes held no traces of merriment. "She is the one who asked you to come."

-ooo-

"We can sit down here and rest a while as we eat. My legs aren't as strong as they once were."

Yesenia followed Tamsin over to two low hassocks set up on rich layers of carpet under a colorful overhead cloth that provided welcome shade. The market kept their environmental controls on the balmy side, likely to encourage just this sort of lazy behavior.

Slow customers saw more to buy.

Fixers, however, couldn't permit their brains to go on vacation—and Yesenia had noted enough on their walk here to have pieced together what she should have known from the first.

Tamsin wasn't just a venerated elder. He was the man in charge.

She sat and waited until he folded his legs into a configuration that would have left her permanently stuck that way, and then handed him one of the two savory pocket pastries she'd been holding.

He set a mug of cider at her right knee and smiled, as if all that mattered in the world was this exact moment and his pleasure in her company.

For a heartbeat, she wished, deeply, that her life

could be so simple—and then she let the weight of all the reasons it couldn't settle back on her shoulders. She'd been born into a hardscrabble existence where a lack of contingency plans got you dead. The hardscrabble part had changed when her Talent had manifested and a very annoyed Seeker had dragged her out of a back alley and into an entirely different life, but Fixers couldn't live entirely in the present moment either, especially the rare ones who could bend space and time and Travel through them both.

"Take a bite. Taste the spices on your tongue. Let yourself have a moment of pleasure, Director."

She hoped her face didn't look as astonished as she felt. Her Talent often let her read minds quite well, but no one ever got much of a glimpse into hers.

Tamsin laughed. "I've been sitting on this hassock longer than you've been alive. There's not much that gets past me."

Too much had been getting past her. She lifted her pastry, thinking. Regardless of who Alara might be, as the leader of this particular enclave of humanity, Tamsin almost certainly had an agenda here. No one would waste a chance to have an audience with the quadrant's highest-ranking KarmaCorp official. She eyed him carefully. "Are you going to tell me what you want now, or are you waiting for the spices to lull me into complacency?"

He shook his head, laughing gently at her again. "I want nothing from you, Traveler, other than that you sit here with me and enjoy some of the finest food in the galaxy and ready your mind and your heart to hear what it is that Alara will tell you."

Her stomach was complaining in at least fifteen languages about the lack of incoming food. "I prefer to hear the pitch directly from the top." She didn't negotiate with underlings.

His eyes looked a little sad. "We don't want anything from you. We seek only to help."

She turned her Talent up several notches and was shocked that it read nothing but absolute sincerity from the man beside her.

"It must be a hard life," he said quietly. "Everyone wanting a piece of you."

The last thing she had expected at an out-of-the-way spaceport was empathy. She set down her uneaten pastry, suddenly shaken, and picked up the cider instead. Its sweetness nearly finished what the old man had started.

She put down the mug sharply. There could be no cracks in the walls of Yesenia Mayes.

His hand settled firmly over hers. "Stay open, mi'dama—no harm will come to you here."

Nobody could promise to keep a Traveler safe. She opened her mouth to say so.

He shook his head, and now his eyes didn't look gentle at all. They looked old and wise and as gnarled and tough as the ages. "Read the energies. You will see that I speak truth."

He knew an awful lot about how her Talent worked. Carefully, without letting down her guard elsewhere, she sent out a questing probe. Calling mostly on her Shaman skills, she felt the ether in the way that was hardest to explain, but for her, easiest to do.

And found what he said she would find. A very clear, very intentional net of safety.

Which was alarming in at least a dozen different ways. She glared at him, KarmaCorp Director in full throttle. "You have a Shaman here?"

"Stand down." His words nearly snapped out. "Respect what you can feel."

She could feel the power in him. Not Talent, but energy. Clarity. Intention. "You have a gift." Something similar, perhaps, to what shamans had been in tribal cultures before KarmaCorp had borrowed the word and given it different meaning.

She had heard quiet whispers of such people—but she had never met someone using their power so openly.

Probably for good reason.

He inclined his head. "Many here see the energies. Some can work with them." He scanned her intently for a moment. "Melessa draws the visions she sees in her dreams."

She cursed herself for missing that, too. If this counted as her inaugural mission as Director, she was making a right mess of things. "Have the Seekers been giving you difficulty?" She hadn't made it to that part of her briefings yet.

"No." He shook his head. "And if they do, we will tell them what we have always told them. Gifts are not Talents. Our children stay with us." His eyes met hers again, solid and strong and making very clear that anyone who disagreed with that would be going through him first.

She had no plans to disagree. The Wanderers had been carefully studied, and they had never produced a rogue Talent. And unlike some of the people of Karma-Corp, she knew better than to believe that they had a monopoly on working with the energies of the universe. However, she spoke as Director now, and while that gave her significant power, it also meant her words would be weighed on a different scale. She considered, and made a decision. "If you have children with Talent, we will welcome them."

He smiled. "Thank you. If we have those who want to come, we will send them."

Good enough. Carefully worded diplomacy on both sides. They understood each other.

She knew that in this, she would differ from the mainstream opinion in the organization she worked for, but that was her right. KarmaCorp was, in the end, no more than the sum total of the people who worked for it, and she did the organization no favors by subsuming anything of who she was simply because it might not be the view in most favor.

Something the man in front of her clearly understood at the level of cloth and weave. She reached for her pastry, feeling more settled than she had since her shuttle set down. "So. Tell me how you became the leader of a tribe of Wanderers that doesn't wander."

His eyes twinkled, and he picked up his own pastry, gesturing it toward hers. "Better ovens."

The surprised laugh escaped before she could catch it—and then the smells under her nose finished the job. Surrendering to what called her, Yesenia leaned in, closed her eyes, and took her first bite.

It was everything the hungry child could have ever wanted it to be. Crispy, flaky crust breaking under her teeth and letting the sopping juices leak through. Pungent spice landing first, and then the rich oils of meat cooked for days in its own juices.

She didn't chew, didn't swallow, didn't move. She just sat, holding that first bite in her mouth and letting the full magic of it work its way loose.

A hum of deep, joyous gratitude rose in her throat, and she let it come. Let the wise old man beside her hear it. Let him see her dancing fingers move to catch the falling flakes of crust and the errant drops trying to run down her chin.

The hungry child, stepping into a moment of utter, sublime perfection.

She heard the soft rumble of laughter beside her. Heard the crunch as Tamsin bit into his own pastry, adding pungent aromas to the already swirling smells.

She didn't say a word—she didn't have to. She just kept eating, one worshipful, intent, delighted mouthful at a time, the fifteen voices in her stomach all rendered speechless.

It had been worth the trip just for this.

-o0o-

"This way, mi'dama."

Yesenia followed, bemused, as the child of the scarves led her down a narrow, twisting row that clearly wasn't where market customers wandered. The girl had shown up just as they were finishing their lunch, bowed, and offered to take their honored visitor to see Alara.

A nice bit of theater, even if she was quite certain it had been scripted.

This part, however, surprised her. People who dared to issue a summons to KarmaCorp personnel generally didn't invite them in the back door.

The girl stopped and glanced over her shoulder, looking a little worried. "Maybe I should have brought you the other way."

Yesenia cursed quietly under her breath and raised her pastry-weakened barriers. Apparently, half the market could read thoughts, and she was broadcasting hers far too loudly. "Are you a sensitive, child?" It seemed politer to ask than to poke at her energetically to find out.

"Maybe." The girl seemed unconcerned. "Alara says that's what the Federation would probably call me. Here, she just tells me I have to be polite and not listen when people are thinking things that are none of my business."

Well, she could approve of Alara that much, at least. Teaching ethics to preteen girls wasn't always easy business, but it was a very necessary one. "Alara is your teacher, then?"

The girl scrunched up her face, apparently in no hurry to keep moving. "Everyone teaches."

Yesenia sighed—she knew better than to impose standard Federation cultural constructs on a group that clearly opted out of most of them. "She helps you learn how to use your gift?"

The child's eyes cleared. "Yes. She helps, and so do Tamsin and Meedan and Geruni and Sam, except Sam can be kind of impatient, so I only go see him when someone else can't help me first because Alara said that would be prudent. I had to look up what that meant on the GooglePlex."

It was impossible not to like the girl, even if she was probably spilling clan secrets as she babbled. "I suspect it's also prudent that you take me to Alara on the quickest path you have available to you."

The child grinned. "I am—that's why I brought you this way. It's messy, but it's a lot faster."

A tribe that fostered independent initiative in their youngest members. Yesenia knew that one of her greatest challenges would be doing the same with the trainees in her care—while making sure they very rarely used it. Talent simply carried too much risk to be given that kind of freedom.

She looked down at her guide, carefree and smiling and swathed in every color of the rainbow, and wondered if the girl had any idea how lucky she was. Raised in a village of plenty with love and guidance at her back.

"I do know." Dark eyes looked up, suddenly very serious. "I'm sorry—I didn't mean to hear that, but you're thinking kind of loudly again."

The many and varied dangers of a full belly. Yesenia

schooled her thoughts to more innocuous things. "Perhaps I need Alara to train me as well."

The child nodded solemnly. "Maybe you do."

Yesenia managed to keep her snort to herself. Nobody trained a Traveler, not a full-grown one, anyhow, but it spoke to the depth of respect for Alara that the child thought she could.

Her guide was on the move again. Yesenia picked her way carefully through ropes and baskets and the colorful riffraff of the part of the market that wasn't usually seen, and spent the journey pulling her full Fixer self back online. She didn't know where she was going quite yet, but she was very sure of one thing.

The crux point of this journey was directly ahead.

-ooo-

"You don't look like a Seer." Yesenia could hear the terseness in her voice—and the nerves. She hoped like hell that the young woman sitting calmly across from her only sensed the former. The lulling effects of spicy pastries and redolent color were long gone.

It was time for business. With a woman who had just proclaimed that she was a Seer in tones most people used to say they were hungry.

"I could, if it would make you feel better." The woman's voice was rich, warm, and amused.

This wasn't about feelings. "You sent me the message."

Shoulders covered in rich purple fabric shrugged negligently. "In a manner of speaking."

The words weren't what Yesenia was focused on, but they annoyed her anyhow. And her Talent wasn't picking up anything that made sense, at least not anything definitive. The woman who had dragged her halfway across the quadrant with a whisper had excellent self-control—and, Yesenia suspected, gifts beyond measure. "Do you have a name?"

"Of course." The woman inclined her head, her tone back to amused. "You may call me Alara."

"That's hardly your full name."

"It's what you're getting."

Not if she could help it. Yesenia switched to a more active probe, sending a light, inaudible series of resonances aimed just under Alara's ribcage. The solar plexus held the seed of who a person was in the world, and Singing Talent was particularly good at reading the energy of the chakras.

For a moment, the notes hung in inaudible space as two strong women looked at each other in a silent contest of wills. And then something flung the fragment of Song away, scattering it as thoroughly as Yesenia had ever seen her Talent tossed.

She blinked, too shocked to be angry. "What are you?"

"Nothing to be probed without consent." There was no amusement now, just the edge of command and steel.

It wasn't a probe of that nature, but Yesenia wasn't

here to debate KarmaCorp ethics. "You sent a three-line message ordering me to show up here at the blasted date and time of your convenience. I have a right to know something about the person who is trying to yank my strings." So far all she had was someone who looked no older than an apprentice Fixer and had a flare for the overly dramatic.

Brown eyes watched her steadily. "You don't like to be ordered around, is that it?"

This was absurd. And potentially dangerous, even if her Talent wasn't sniffing so much as a whiff of current threat. Outside the tent, the market proceeded as always, with nary a ripple of concern from the hundreds of people in attendance. Yesenia reached a little farther, but didn't detect anything that would suggest the more focused intent of someone looking to do harm, especially the kind of skilled someone who would need to be sent to deal with a Fixer of legend.

The Federated Commonwealth of Planets wasn't a fertile breeding ground for assassins, but she'd met a few in her time. None of them had been foolish enough to get in her way.

"One day you will need to learn to trust."

Yesenia's eyes shot back to Alara's face, which suddenly seemed hidden in shadows. "Is that prophecy, Seer, or mere guesswork?"

"Some of both."

Her Talent was reading only honest intent. Whatever the uncommon young woman on the other side of the table was, she believed herself to be telling the truth.

"I would appreciate it if we could dispense with the theater and get to the point."

The young Seer smiled. "Sadly, the universe doesn't always speak as clearly as both of us would wish."

She wasn't here for platitudes, even ones delivered with wry wisdom. "It apparently spoke clearly enough for you to feel justified in summoning me away from my duties." The sheer arrogance of that still astonished KarmaCorp's newest director. "Do you have any idea how much work awaits me?"

"No." Alara seemed unconcerned by the specter of piles of paperwork or powerful people kept waiting. "I know that the energies move strongly around you."

That much Yesenia had known since she was eight years old and time had started rippling as she slept. "KarmaCorp is aware of that, as am I."

The Seer bowed her head slightly. "KarmaCorp is respected here."

It was—but it wasn't revered. Or feared. What lived here stood apart and felt itself equal, and so far, Yesenia hadn't seen anything to lead her to dispute that. There was power here, and control, and wisdom.

Alara's lips quirked, as if she heard the unspoken thoughts. "I expected it to be harder to convince you of that."

Yesenia felt the opening and stepped into it. "I have a Talent that in almost any other age would have made me a sorceress."

The Seer nodded. "Amongst my people, we would call you that still."

The Anthros would have a field day here—assuming they were ever let in the door. "I do not dismiss knowledge gained through unusual means." She simply had high standards for what qualified as knowledge.

That part wasn't necessary to say. Someone as self-confident as the woman before her would take it as a given.

The young Seer met her gaze for a long moment, and then nodded again and steepled her hands in front of her face. A decision made. "I know this much. I have seen your face in my dreaming for nigh on ten years now. I didn't know who you were until I sat watching a vid one night with my niece and nephew and you showed up in a news clip. It was right after you'd returned from Halcyon Omega."

The mission that had made her a household name on far too many planets. "If you're looking for a piece of fame and fortune, you're welcome to all of them."

"I imagine they aren't a comfortable weight to carry for one who seeks to live in the shadows."

Yesenia didn't want to know if that was prophecy or guesswork. Too many people here understood her far too well. She had very little experience with being transparent. "I seek to do my job."

"You do it well. I believe that will continue." Alara paused, and for the first time, gave off faint flickers of unease. "It is your personal life that will tangle and bring you grief."

That wasn't possible. "I don't *have* a personal life."

"That is a sadness."

She wasn't here for counseling. "I have a shuttle to catch, and you're wasting my time."

Alara sat up, both hands on the table, eyes full of snapping light. Suddenly, she looked every bit a Seer. "I will excuse your rudeness, Yesenia Mayes, for I have seen your tears and your anguish and your terrible loneliness."

Something bleak and hard came to life in Yesenia's gut right underneath her solar plexus.

"You will find love," said the Seer softly, every word liquid fire. "And then it will be ripped away from you. The one because you must let it go, and the other because you choose it."

The heart Yesenia claimed she didn't have squeezed tightly. "Why?"

"I don't know. I don't believe I am meant to see what happens." Alara clasped her hands together slowly. "I am only meant to deliver you this message. To save the ones you love, you must find the four."

"Four what?" So far, this was a Gordian knot of gibberish.

"I don't know." Alara's eyes cleared, full of sharp intelligence now—and empathy. "I only know that every morning of the last ten years that I have woken with your face in my mind, it has come with those three words. *Find the four.*"

"Then you've spent ten years wasting your time." Yesenia could hear the sharpness of her tone, a knife's edge trying to wield certainty where none existed.

"You have Shaman Talent." Alara's fingers traced the lines of the largest of her rings.

All Travelers did. "I have all four of the Talents."

"Then you know that these energies are both imprecise and important."

They were—if Alara was anything more than a highly skilled charlatan.

The woman across the table smiled. "Believe as you must. I've done what the spirits have asked me to do, and that is enough. I trust that if you need my words, you will remember them."

She wasn't likely to forget. Not when something deep inside her own soul knew them for truth, as wildly annoying and inconvenient as that might be. And that meant she couldn't walk out of here a Fixer in high dudgeon, even if every fiber of her being wanted to do just that.

Yesenia Mayes honored truth, even when it was difficult. She bowed her head in the mannerisms of her youth. "I thank you."

Brown eyes sparked with surprise. And then a corner of Alara's mouth turned up. "You are not what I expected, Traveler."

That went both ways. "Nor are you, Seer."

Yesenia stood up, feeling the energies abruptly release.

Alara stayed seated, hands flat on the table. "Are you headed back to your shuttle? I can have someone walk with you."

The oddest energy seized Yesenia, tickling her insides and making her want to sneeze. "I believe I have a stop or two to make first." She had a tube of drawings to pick up

—and one final errand she was taking pains not to examine too carefully.

She assumed she wouldn't have any difficulty finding the young girl with the bright eyes and the gaudy scarves. She had no truck with scarves, and she didn't intend to start now.

But perhaps her new office could use a rug.

AN ASSISTANT AS ORDERED

"NAME?"

Bean looked down at her travel-worn shirtsleeves and tried to remember if she'd left Gastonia with all her body parts, much less a name. And whether she wanted her new life in this new place to begin with a label from the old one.

Then again, telling the customs people a name that didn't match her ident card was probably a guaranteed trip to a small room and lots of frowning, at the very least, and she didn't have the patience or the emotional energy to deal with either. "Lucinda Coffey."

"Planet of origin?"

She held her breath and kept telling the truth. "Gastonia."

The agent's eyebrow went up. "And when was the last time you were home?"

They'd be used to inner-planet travelers here. That much was obvious from the relaxed stance of the official security types she'd laid eyes on and the lack of blasters, hidden or otherwise. This was a place that trusted that things usually went according to plan and that new arrivals were generally nice people. Nothing lax about the security, but the vibe was different from what she was used to.

Not that Gastonia was overflowing with official security types. "I've lived there off and on my whole life." That much they'd be able to read from her ident card, although it didn't have a record of all her comings and goings. "Most recently, I was off-world to attend higher education training in business systems." That had been a cover story, but today it was probably going to be a useful one.

The woman on the other side of the counter raised an eyebrow.

Bean knew why. Dreadlocked hair, iridescent skin-suit, and enough jewelry to start up a market stand. She didn't look like a tech geek.

The agent pulled up a screen on the big monitor and manual keyboard system she used. Old school. Bean approved. Tablets were good for all kinds of things, but they made your eyes cross after a while.

Bean took the time to glance at the name stitched on the agent's navy-blue skinsuit. Ophelia. She grinned— that was almost as bad as Lucinda.

The agent looked up in time to catch the grin and the direction Bean's eyes were pointing. "Tell me about it. My mom is a professor of ancient poetry. There was just no way I was getting born with a name that wasn't embarrassing."

And yet she'd had it stitched onto her skinsuit. Ophelia Barnes clearly loved her mother. "Most people call me Bean."

Ophelia grinned. "Better than Lucy, huh?"

On a rough-and-tumble world like Gastonia, you didn't give people a really obvious reason to pick on you. "Did you stick with Ophelia?"

"Only for work." The agent smiled, her eyes friendlier now. "It makes people underestimate me."

Which probably wasn't something she told most people standing on the other side of her counter. "I bet."

Ophelia glanced back at the paperwork. "Why'd you leave Gastonia?"

For a lot of reasons that wouldn't be in the paperwork. Bean considered and discarded the sanitized story she'd made up in the shuttle exit tunnel. She generally preferred to live her life telling as much of the truth as possible. "Pissed off the wrong people."

"They have a thing against business systems?"

The agent's voice was mildly amused, but Bean didn't miss the new sharpness in her eyes. Stardust Prime might be a more relaxed world, but it wasn't a sloppy one. "They have a thing against people who don't dance to the beat of their drum. Nothing illegal."

Ophelia tapped away on her keyboard. "You wouldn't have gotten the paperwork to travel here if it had been."

Now wasn't the time to draw attention to her skills in

procuring the impossible. And she was really hoping that she might be able to start a life here where that wasn't her most valued skill.

The agent was looking up again. "Why Stardust Prime?"

That was a lot trickier. "I'm looking for work." Which was the absolute truth, but only the tiniest tip of it.

"With these papers, you could have gone to any inner-planet world you liked. Lots of them where you could have had a job in business systems before you got off the shuttle."

Bean tried another small dose of truth and gestured at her dreadlocked hair and rainbow headscarf. "I wanted a place where I maybe didn't have to lose all this to get work." Inner planets welcomed diversity and flamboyant personalities, but generally not in their systems techs.

Not that she was a very good systems tech anyhow. She'd been too busy trying to find the Gastonia leader's missing nephew to pay much attention to her classes. Which was a story she couldn't tell, because finding Antonio and then giving him extra lessons in how to stay better hidden was why she needed to keep far away from Gastonia for a while.

Probably a lifetime length of a while. She swallowed. She'd made the choice to pay this price weeks ago. Now she just needed to get on with it.

The agent typed a couple of things on her keyboard and surveyed the screen, chewing her bottom lip. "You've got no criminal, decent education, a little shy on employment history, but enough." She looked down at the paperwork one last time and then up at Bean again. "There are jobs to be had here so long as there aren't any big flags in your file, and I don't see any. Should I?"

The big events of Bean's life didn't tend to quantify well for the ident files. "No."

"Okay." Something in Ophelia's eyes spoke of kindness. "Your paperwork is all in order, then. Welcome to Stardust Prime."

"Excellent." Bean let a little of her relief show on her face. "Know a good place to catch a bite to eat?"

"Yup. Got a tablet? It's a little hard to find, so I'll do you a map."

Bean pulled out her ancient and sturdy Anzer. She had a fancier model tucked away in her bag, but it had toys on it she didn't want anyone accidentally swiping.

The agent smirked. "You might want to upgrade your equipment if you want systems-tech work."

Bean grinned. "Keeping this old guy running is a pretty good demonstration of my skills, don't you think?"

Ophelia laughed. "You have a point." She tapped a couple of times on the old tablet and placed a pin on a map. "Jissa's diner is here—you can get there on foot in about ten minutes. Tell her I sent you, and ask for pie, even if it isn't on the menu today."

Bean knew gold when she heard it. "Awesome, thanks."

A small pause, and then Ophelia shrugged. "You might not thank me for this one, but I hear Yesenia Mayes is looking for a new assistant."

"Again?" The agent in the next cubicle rolled his

eyes. "That makes, what—six that she's chewed up and spit out this rotation already?"

"Seven. The one before this barely made it in her office door, but she got hired, so it counts." Bean's minder shook her head. "You couldn't make me work for that woman for all the chocolate in the quadrant."

That was a pretty warn-off—but it was also a line on a potential job, and recently arrived unemployeds from Gastonia knew better than to walk away from those. "How would I go about applying for this position?"

Surprised green eyes studied her from the cubicle next door.

Bean grimaced—if she'd been trying to slide through quietly, apparently being willing to take a job in the lion's den wasn't the way to do it.

"Take it from me." The suddenly friendly agent in the adjoining cubicle leaned over and pitched his voice at barely more than a whisper. "Walk around a bit, scan the wanteds for a couple of weeks—you'll find something. No need to let Yesenia Mayes chomp you."

No one got to take a chunk out of Bean unless she wanted them to, but friendly warnings weren't something she was in the habit of ignoring. "Got it, thanks."

Ophelia just smiled.

Two women with floofy names, smart enough not to underestimate each other. Bean nodded her thanks and picked up her tablet and paperwork off the counter.

Time to go find some pie—and to figure out why she was supposed to be here.

-ooo-

It was the sort of diner that could make the right kind of person feel at home anywhere in the universe.

Bean was the right kind of person. Jissa's establishment had been exactly where Ophelia had put it on the map, tucked into a side street that said the locals knew where to find it and that was plenty of business to keep the proprietor happy.

Jissa herself was currently waiting tables, filling coffee mugs, and chatting with the regulars. If Bean had caught the diurnal cycle information on the shuttle right, it was mid-afternoon. One rush done and another coming, but in the meantime, life could move along slow and comfortable. Which suited everyone in the place except for possibly Bean's belly, but she knew how to wait out hunger. There was a plate of all-day breakfast on the way and pie after that, and after a week of shuttle rations, her whole body was going to sit up and sing hallelujah when they arrived.

Especially when Jissa had whispered that she had real eggs today, same price as the regular breakfast plate.

There was just no way the woman made any money doing that, but Bean wasn't an idiot. She'd ordered the eggs, and tossed a thought of gratitude the way of the customs agent who had probably gotten her into the line for them. Jissa clearly liked Ophelia, and dropping her name had smoothed things in a way that Bean had to appreciate.

Smoothing had pretty much been her life's work up until now.

Which had her all kinds of curious about why the tug in her gut had been pulling her inexorably toward this planet for the last two months. She could already tell just how different it was from Gastonia, including the friendly people and promising offerings on the food front. How she fit here wasn't at all clear yet, despite the rumblings in her gut that said she'd arrived.

Maybe her gut was just hungry.

Or maybe it didn't know that Gastonia's best greaser was in retirement, effective immediately.

Which chased right back around to the niggling issue of needing to find alternative employment. Bean looked up as the diner's proprietor meandered her way. Jissa seemed like the friendly type, and also like one of those people who knew a little bit about everything. Bean swallowed another sip of still-piping-hot coffee and pitched her voice low enough to at least try to keep her business quiet. "Do you happen to know where I might find a woman named Yesenia Mayes?"

The comfortably middle-aged woman's eyes widened. "Director Mayes? You got business with her?"

Possibly. "What's she the Director of?"

"Officially she runs KarmaCorp in this quadrant." Jissa raised a wry eyebrow. "Unofficially, honey, she runs everything that breathes here on Stardust Prime."

And evidently ate assistants for breakfast while she did it. Which, Bean well knew, should have her running for the hills or the nearest temp agency. But despite her general lack of willingness to sit in places previous tenants had vacated in pieces, something about this job was part of the tugging. She knew a little about Karma-Corp. A power in the galaxy, at least in places where the cartels didn't run things. "She's got a heavy hand?"

A thoughtful pause. "Not a light one, but she's fair. Hard, though. You never see that one smiling."

An interesting mix of scuttlebutt. "Is the whole company that way, or just her?" Maybe she could slide in somewhere a little less close to the lion's den.

Jissa's eyes softened. "Nah, KarmaCorp's good people. They make things right out there in the galaxy, and when they've got their feet on-planet, they make good neighbors." She winked. "And big tippers."

Huh. That kind of corporate culture generally had a source. Which meant it either went through Yesenia Mayes, or around her. "The boss lady—has she ever been in here?"

"Not on my watch." Jissa cast a quick glance sideways, like someone might be listening in. "But she came in once with one of the shuttle captains. Ordered a latte and tore a strip up one side of him and down the other and then tossed him down the compost chute. Least that's the way I heard it from Ellie, and she heard it from Jules, who was on night shift and heard every word."

For the first time since she'd landed on Stardust Prime, Bean felt entirely at home. On Gastonia, gossip was the universal currency, and a good greaser's very best friend.

Just one of the things that wasn't in her official ident

file. "What'd the shuttle captain do wrong?" No guarantee that had been the direction of guilt, but she had a feeling.

"Gave one of her Fixers grief for puking on his bridge. One of the young ones, out in the field for the first time." Jissa's tone was almost motherly. "They tend to overdo it out there the first trip or two."

The only Fixer Bean had ever come anywhere near had impressed the hell out of her—and seemed the most unlikely person in the universe to have hurled where someone else could see. "She got space sick?"

"Yup. She was a Grower, and they don't like having their hands and feet away from the dirt."

Bean was taking mental notes as fast as she could write them. "And Director Mayes went after the captain." Not the greenie Fixer, which is what most would have done.

Jissa nodded, face full of curiosity. "Why you asking?"

It was apparently a day for telling the truth to strangers. Bits of it, anyhow. "I heard she was hiring. Looking for an assistant."

"Phew." Brown eyes contemplated for a moment. "She'd be a hard one to work for."

That much had come through loud and clear. "I don't mind hard."

"Fair enough." Jissa waved over a server carrying the plate of all-day breakfast, and let her settle it in front of Bean. Then she waited a moment as the server hustled off and Bean picked up her fork. "I could use someone for extra shifts on the weekend. If things don't work out with the boss lady."

Bean looked up, evaluating the offer—and decided it was real. Real, and generally the kind of thing she would have snapped up in a heartbeat. But it didn't have the tug. "Thanks. I'll keep that in mind."

Jissa smiled and picked up her coffee pot, wandering in the direction of two older men with dirt on their hands.

Bean put her fork to good use and dug into the best meal she'd had in a lot longer than two months. Whoever raised the chickens that laid these eggs knew what they were doing, and the rest of the plate did the eggs proud.

It wasn't until a piece of pie the size of her head arrived that she contemplated the tug again. And decided, very sadly, that it wasn't pulling her to weekends working in Jissa's diner. She'd just have to make do with being a customer. A very regular customer, if the pleasure seeping through her veins was any kind of judge.

Bean stood up—there was work to do before she let that pie put her to sleep. She reached for her bag and tossed some credits on the table. A lot of them. She might not be an official greaser anymore, but old habits weren't going to die anytime soon.

Jissa, swinging by with her coffee pot, took one look and rolled her eyes. "That's about five times what's reasonable, honey."

Not today, it wasn't. "Some's for you. Some's to pay for Ophelia's next piece of pie."

The rest of it was to pay for the answers the past hour had given. She was close now—and fueled up on eggs, pie, and the beginnings of a sense that she could find a place for herself here.

For the first time in two months, Lucinda Coffey was maybe finally heading toward something.

-ooo-

For a major power in the universe, KarmaCorp's offices didn't run to swanky. Bean followed the directions she'd been given by more than one helpful person, working her way through the interesting mix of town and colony and working farm that was the populated part of Stardust Prime.

KarmaCorp Headquarters was a low, angular building on a campus that apparently included residential components, a school, research facilities, and some of the prettiest gardens Bean had seen anywhere.

Inside, the corridors were that same blend of nondescript and touches of the personal. The walls were the basic plastic of institutional everywhere, although she liked the vaguely turquoise color. The floors and lighting were basic and functional, with pops of color and art in the occasional alcove. Welcome and ease and the clear statement that results, preferably of the non-flashy kind, mattered here—but so did beauty.

Bean liked it very much. A person could be comfortable here.

Which didn't fit with what she'd heard about the woman in the top office at all.

She made her way closer to the inner sanctum, where

the nice gentleman who had greeted her when she'd entered the building had assured her she would find the Director's office.

Bean hadn't stated her business, and the friendly gentleman hadn't asked. One gatekeeper bypassed, and likely the easiest. She'd need to find her way around the rest, however many there were. Presumably, Yesenia Mayes would find that a key qualification in anyone she hired to man her own gate.

In the end, assistant was just a more polite name for a greaser, or at least that was the way Bean was going to play it.

When she finally got to the end of the hall and stepped into a semi-circular space with a partly open sliding door in the back wall, she knew she'd arrived. She also knew the place was empty. People with power had a certain feel, and you didn't last long on Gastonia unless you knew how to smell that vibe.

What you did after that depended on a whole lot of factors.

Bean stood still and surveyed what she could see, contemplating her options.

That the space was empty and unguarded spoke volumes about the woman who generally hung out in the back office. Most people would assume it meant Yesenia Maye's power was absolute, and no one dared cross her. Bean knew enough of power to sniff something different here.

Whatever scuttlebutt might say, the Director trusted her people.

The feeling that had been coalescing in Bean's belly since she stepped off the shuttle got a little sturdier. Despite obvious outward appearances, she could work here.

Her lips twitched as she surveyed the outer office again. That work started with what was in front of her eyes, because right now this space said a whole bunch of things it probably shouldn't. The single console desk in the room was modern and functional, with a couple of dents to make it interesting. The chair behind it sat empty and forlorn, the seat a little lopsided, like the last occupant had just kind of slid off the side instead of exiting on their feet.

Given what she'd heard so far, that wasn't a totally unlikely scenario.

Other than that, the small reception area had about as much personality as a packet of slightly stale soup crackers. Clearly, no one had lived here long enough to make their mark—from what Bean could see, no one had even put up a decent fight.

She knew how to fight.

Curious now, she stepped forward. The Director almost certainly hadn't left her door cracked open by accident, and Bean had never apologized for using her eyes.

What she could see wasn't nearly as boring as the bland space she stood in. It wasn't decorated to Bean's taste, but it spoke vividly of the woman who ruled from within those four walls.

A gleaming desk that was almost certainly wood, and

told the story of unwavering certainty in every line. The large black chair behind it was a seat of power in every way possible. A tablet neatly positioned for actual work, windows that let light fill every corner of the room, and the briefest glance of an inbuilt wall of equipment that would put most of the power brokers on Gastonia to absolute shame.

It wasn't the tech that had Bean riveted, however. It was the flowers. And the rug.

The flowers were spectacular—red and bold and daring the eye to look anywhere else. Their color was echoed in the simple rag rug on the floor in front of the desk, one that had clearly come from a weaver skilled in both choice of fabric and use of color. From Andea, maybe, or Tezuli. It was stunning, and at first look, it didn't fit the rest of the office at all.

Anyone who thought that was a fool. Bean was pretty sure that rug spoke more truth than everything else inside those four walls. Yesenia Mayes needed an assistant who understood that—and who supported the way the Director wanted the world to see her anyhow.

Bean sighed. She knew where she needed to be now. One look at that rug and she was a goner.

Convincing the woman who owned the rug was a different matter entirely—but that was the kind of work a good greaser knew how to do.

Bean shimmied left foot to right a couple of times, thinking. And then made a decision. If she was going around gatekeepers, she might as well circumvent them all.

Including the one at the top.

She spun around on her heels. It was going to cost most of what she had left in her pockets to do this right, and if Stardust Prime ran to the usual diurnal schedules, most of what she needed was going to be locked away for the night soon.

Bean cast one last look over her shoulder as she left and smiled at the frayed corner of the rug on the Director's floor.

Yup, this one was calling to her.

-ooo-

The footsteps in the hallway were all the warning Bean had. Just enough time to gulp, pray, and set down her coffee cup.

The woman who strode into the reception area was a force of nature in every sense of the word. Wild black hair, flashing brown eyes, and a red skinsuit that said she might sit behind a desk now, but she hadn't started there.

Bean tried hard not to contemplate where the seven previous occupants of her chair had ended up.

Director Mayes made it almost to the door of her office before she seemed to realize Bean was there. She turned sharply, and there was real menace in her gaze. "Who are you?"

Show time.

Bean stood up, holding up a mug in one hand, a carafe of coffee in the other. Jissa had done her a solid on the coffee connection. She'd found the mugs in a dusty back corner of the thrift store that had also produced the abstract wall hangings, the set of tribal drums, and the cool set of curled branches that she'd managed to turn into a plant stand overnight with the application of enough wire and persistence.

Yesenia was staring at the small drum on the edge of Bean's console like it might explode. Then her eyes traveled the rest of the room in a quick, precise pattern that said the woman missed nothing and formed her opinions at the speed of light. When she made it back to Bean, the menace had congealed into something far scarier.

Willing her hands not to shake and her bracelets not to jangle, Bean poured. It wasn't just a matter of pride—she'd spent every last credit she had furnishing the office she intended to make her own. Should that insane gamble fail, as all present indicators seemed to suggest, this might be the last real coffee she drank for quite a while.

When the cup was mostly full, she offered it Yesenia's direction. "Best beans I could find on short notice." Prepared black, which, as far as anyone knew, was the way the Director liked it. Scuttlebutt on her tastes had been surprisingly scarce. "I'm your new assistant, at least until you decide to toss me down the compost chute like the last guy, or find someone better. My name's Lucinda Coffey, but everyone calls me Bean."

For a long, terrifying moment, nothing in the room moved.

And then a glimmer of something that might almost be amusement glinted in brown eyes. "The last guy couldn't have found the compost chute with a gold-plated map and a platoon of guides."

Ouch. "I'm pretty good with finding things."

Yesenia took three steps forward, reached for the mug in Bean's left hand, and sniffed. Her right eyebrow lifted. "You apparently found decent coffee."

She owed Jissa. Big. "I can have you better within a week."

This time, Yesenia's eyes traveled over Bean's person. "You don't look remotely like an assistant."

One more time, Bean prayed and took a gamble. "That won't change. I don't shift my skin for anyone. What you see is what you get."

Brown eyes flashed steel—and then that stealthy sense of amusement again. "What makes you think that won't get you a quick ride down a compost chute?"

A lot of things, but she wasn't prepared to talk about most of them yet. "One, you need a body in this chair so you can get your job done, and how I look has nothing to do with whether or not I can deliver. Two, people are going to talk about me, and if they're talking about my hair or my drums or my parrot collection, they're not talking about how long it might be until you fire me. And three, I've heard that you're tough as nails, hell on incompetence, and demanding as a palace full of virgin queens, but I've never heard anyone say you were petty."

Yesenia lifted her mug of coffee slowly and took a sip. "You have a parrot collection?"

Bean grinned. "Not yet."

The Director glanced at the small, beat-up tablet on the console. "How are your tech skills?"

That was a throwaway question. She'd be fired in ten minutes if she didn't have them. "Good enough."

Yesenia took another sip from her coffee. "Our incoming class of trainees arrived two weeks ago. One of the girls is from a large family on Effusia, and she's very homesick. If I made it your job to help her feel more comfortable here, what would you do?"

Not a throwaway question. Effusia was one of the inner planets, with a tight, clan-based social system. Bean tried to imagine what it might feel like to be thrown out of that into a school where you knew no one and no one knew your family. "I'd check and make sure that the people who generally work with the trainees had tried all the usual things, like rearranging her room to feel more like home and helping her make a friend or two. Then I'd take a guess that she needs more of a social structure than a cohort of ten-year-old girls and see if I could find a local family that might be willing to informally adopt her."

The Director raised an eyebrow. "And at what point in that would you consult with me?"

Bean held in her sigh of relief. Gastonia's best greaser knew when she was making progress. "When I failed or when I succeeded." No way this woman wanted an assistant who needed to be micromanaged.

Brown eyes pinned her like a flapping moth. "Do you fail often?"

Depended who you asked. "No."

Another slow sip of coffee, and then Yesenia turned

toward her office door. She looked back over her shoulder and offered up a regal nod. "You can stay. For now. I'll let you know when I've found someone better."

Bean managed to keep her grin fairly subdued. "I'll make sure I know the way to the nearest compost chute."

The Director's lips almost twitched. "See that you do."

A TALE OF TWO SHIPS

SHE WAS DEAD.

Sigrid Albrecht snatched her face off the console that had apparently turned into a pillow for her latest desperate catnap. Every damn alarm on the *Skrapp* was sounding, even a couple she knew hadn't worked for at least a decade.

All letting her know the obvious. Her old, leaky nav charts had been wrong. There weren't clear skies out this side of the Veridian ice fields—there was a fucking huge rock. And she had solar sails in full deployment.

Turning while deployed was suicide—it would rip the ship in half.

152 seconds until impact.

Her brain, suffering from traumatic lack of sleep, still had no problem doing that math. 2.5 minutes left to live.

Sigrid stabbed at buttons, ignoring the wailing behind her. Freja would just have to wait.

Freja.

Sigrid's heart clutched. Her precious baby girl. Everything else in her life had been mercilessly snatched away, and now it seemed the universe was coming for her tiny daughter too.

It hadn't even waited a week.

She banged her right hand on two different consoles, trying to quiet the damn alarms. Her left hand abused the sonar, radar, nav charts. Trying to find a way to take a crippled junker around a freaking huge asteroid.

One that wasn't supposed to be there.

131 seconds.

She should have bought better charts, but charts cost money, and there had been precious little of that lately. She'd needed the cash off this trip. Pickings had been good—not a lot of junkers collected in this sector. She had a cargo hold full of high-quality space trash.

It would form her burial mound.

117 seconds.

Freja's wailing pierced through the alarms. Sigrid glanced over at the tiny, mad arms flailing at the monstrous sounds that had invaded newborn sleep and felt her heart split in two. She'd never know now if her girl was going to have her momma's straight blonde hair or the curls of the man who had accidentally helped to make her.

Apparently black market fertility control wasn't any better than black market nav charts.

Sigrid looked back at her consoles. It was bleak. She could slow the *Skrapp* down a little. Enough to maybe leave their dead bodies intact instead of pulverized into ooze.

Long enough for the sky gods to find her tiny girl's soul.

101 seconds.

She'd always had a weakness for the gods. It wasn't reciprocal. They'd never noticed she existed.

Freja. Named for the Norse goddess of love and beauty—and of death. It had been the name that had come to Sigrid as she lay curled up on a pallet, exhausted and alone, after giving birth in the *Skrapp's* cargo hold. The med bot had died right about the time her water had broken. Which was fine, because Sigrid had been about to strangle it anyhow. No damn bot got to tell her how to breathe.

82 seconds.

Breathing. Oxygen. The cargo hold had an evac pod. A junked one she'd scooped up in an asteroid field three days before Freja's birth—and hooked up to her systems long enough to verify its life support still worked.

Worth more that way.

Sigrid bolted for the port to her cargo hold. The evac pod wouldn't fly, and she didn't have a door to push it out of, but it was a tough, padded cylinder. One with oxygen.

The closest she could come to a womb on short notice.

No time.

She reversed herself back through the port hole and grabbed Freja, wrapped in a batik scarf and remnants of an old skinsuit. Poor kid. She'd had a weird life in her six days in the galaxy.

Fortunately, the med bot's single auto-diaper had still been functional.

61 seconds.

Sigrid kissed the top of her daughter's head and propelled them both into the cargo hold. She tucked Freja into the evac pod, batik scarf and all. And then, heart rending, touched one finger to her sweet girl's red, yowling cheek and slammed the door of the small capsule shut.

Two steps and she had both hands on the cargo hold console. It worked better than most on the ship, and it would let her spend the last 61 seconds of her life close enough to see her baby girl through the evac pod's tiny window.

Frantically she re-programmed the code, running shunts around the systems that were already broken and the ones unlikely to survive impact.

Impact. She couldn't think about that now.

46 seconds.

Sigrid's fingers flew, echoes of when she'd been one of the best programmers in the Federation's fleet. Before Antonio. Before the handsome man who had pulled her over to the dark side.

Before she'd sold her soul to try and save him.

Her luck with men had never changed—Brag had only been the latest. Named after the Viking god of music and poetry, and he'd been a master of both. His voice had seduced her in one long, slow evening over mugs of spiced mead in between sets at the bar on Heimili Station.

A bard with a golden voice. Maybe his daughter had inherited some of his fortune.

She would need it.

22 seconds.

Sigrid cursed and locked in the last two lines of code. All oxygen would route to the evac pod on impact.

Which would likely only mean that her beautiful, innocent, defenseless baby girl would die slowly and alone on the side of an unforgiving astral rock.

Sigrid's eyes filled with hot tears. She slashed them away with the back of her hand, knowing she had to be able to see. Had to time the execution of the code just right, or *Skrapp's* sense of self-preservation would override the suicide script.

8 seconds.

She watched the view screen and the oncoming, rushing horror of the rock. Watched the evil numbers counting down, her finger hovering over the execute command. Looked one last time at the red, screaming face of her tiny girl, about to be birthed yet again into an unfriendly world.

And pushed the button.

-ooo-

Eight Years Later...

"Hey, kiddo. Keep it under three gees, okay?"

Lakisha Drinkwater, eight and already one of the best pilots on Halkyn VII, rolled her eyes. "I can fly faster than that and you know it."

Her father ruffled her blonde, wavy hair. "I know. But the pressure hull can't handle it."

She sighed. "Is the patch failing again?" That meant they'd be grounded until they could borrow Tivi Malcolm's blow torch. Which, given how mad he was at the Drinkwaters right now, might be a while.

Everyone was kind of mad at the Drinkwaters. Her oldest brother Jingo was the newest full-fledged digger on the rock, and he'd been assigned the pile-of-crap shaft to mine. Or at least, that's what everyone had called it until he'd found the vein of iridium in the back right corner.

Iridium was the most valuable thing they mined in this sector, and a new vein would earn a hefty finder's bonus. Maybe Jingo could buy them a blow torch.

Whatever. Kish's mind swerved away from the boring issues of iridium and money and petty digger-rock politics and surveyed the horizon. It was a big treat to be out here, and she wasn't going to let anything distract her for a second. Even if she had to fly at the speed of a slow turtle.

She glanced over at the man in the co-pilot seat. Pops looked happy. There was no one better in the driver's seat of a flitter, but that wasn't the reason she'd been willing to get up before skybreak to come flying with him.

Out here, he treated her like an equal—or at least like someone who might be worth his while one day. At home, she was just the smallest and scrappiest of eight kids, and if she got noticed, it was usually because she was in trouble. Again.

There were a lot of ways to get in trouble on a digger rock when your heart yearned to be somewhere else and there was nowhere else to go.

Kish looked out at the stars and wished, like she always did, that the clunky old tin can under her hands could carry her there.

"Don't be wishing for what you can't have." Her dad's voice was gruff, and a little impatient—they'd had this conversation before.

She could feel her lower lip popping out. "It doesn't hurt anything to look." But it did. She could see the small caldera coming over the horizon—the one that marked the spot where they'd found her DNA mother's ship.

The man who had rescued a squalling baby out of an evac pod and taken her home laid his hand on her shoulder. "Head right, kiddo. No time for sightseeing today. We need to run the lines. If we're not back by dinner, your mom will make us eat cold potato flakes."

That wasn't much worse than having to eat them warm. Payday for Pops was still four days away, and there would be a lot of potato flakes between now and then. And soy paste.

Kish scowled. She *hated* soy paste. She banked carefully to starboard—it wasn't a hard maneuver, but the left thruster had been acting up lately, and if she broke that, they'd definitely be grounded. She hummed a little to the flitter under her breath.

"Stop with yer singing already. It's a machine, not a baby."

Pops sounded annoyed. She glanced over at him, hoping he was just teasing.

He winked at her. "Think you can hold that patch on with a little ditty, do you?"

Not likely—but sometimes she thought her singing made Pops happier. Even when he scowled. Kish kept humming and swept her eyes over the instrument panel with a practiced gaze. Everything was good except for the auto-stabilizer, and that had been broken since she was three.

Fortunately, Kish had an iron stomach—so long as she didn't feed it soy paste.

She jumped as the radio squawked and dumped out a bunch of gibberish.

"Damn." Pops leaned forward, tension in his voice. "I thought Jingo fixed this thing."

Kish gripped the yoke under her hands until her knuckles turned white. They always left the flitter radio on the emergency frequency. Chatter on that channel meant something had exploded or someone was dead.

Or both.

Pops jimmied with the radio controls, trying to get a better signal. The squawking got louder—and then suddenly cleared. "... the Federated Commonwealth of Planets trader ship *Ios*. We have crashed and need immediate assistance. Repeat—we have crashed and need immediate assistance."

Kish and her dad gaped at the radio.

"We caught their signal. We must be close." Pops yanked an ancient pair of binoculars out of the net above his head and jammed them against his eyes. "Take her up. Now. Fast and hard."

He wasn't Pops now. Those were the terse orders of one of Halkyn VII's finest first responders.

Kish's chest nearly blew up with pride. He was letting her fly. In an emergency. Only the best pilots got to do that. She pointed the flitter's nose almost straight up. Height first —Pops needed visibility. The old machine stuttered, but it went up. Kish pushed a little more, and started to sing.

The stutters evened out a little. She watched the rising coolant temperature—much higher, and they'd have impeller issues.

Pops still had his binoculars glued to the window. "Nothing. Swing right. Head past that caldera first—I want to see the far side."

Kish gulped and headed straight for the place where her DNA mother had died. No one ever went there. Ghosts. Bad juju. Darkside cold.

A flash out the left window caught her attention. "Pops. Over here."

He swung himself to the other side of the flitter in one quick motion. "Where? I don't see it."

She didn't either—not anymore. But something inside her knew where it had come from. "I know where to go."

Kish wrenched at the controls, suddenly frantic. In an emergency, speed mattered. Seconds mattered. People died in seconds.

Pops said nothing. He just stared out the window.

Kish couldn't look—she had her hands full holding the flitter steady. But she could feel the right way to go. There was a rope now, reeling her in.

His harsh intake of breath confirmed what she already knew. "Over there, by the rift." He glanced at her, eyes grim, assessing. "Take us down."

Her chest puffed again, even as her heart pounded against her ribs. This was what it felt like to be important. This was what it felt like to matter.

-ooo-

Amelie Descol blasted the single high, pure note into every nook and cranny of the devastated bridge—and knew she was fighting a losing battle.

She gathered her breath and pushed more power into the single frequency. Sustaining. Demanding. Trying to snatch victory from the jaws of defeat. Her Talent shrieked, protesting the abuse. This wasn't sustainable, even for one of KarmaCorp's very finest.

She knew what her Talent didn't. This was the end game, one way or the other. If she couldn't hold on until help arrived, this was her last Song.

And the likelihood of help arriving in time had narrowed down to one small blip. They had a signal-obliterating cosmic storm behind them and a MayDay beacon that had deked left when it should have gone right. Amelie watched the bridge's last functional view screen as the tiny ship they'd picked up on their sensors came into view.

Her heart lurched. It was a surface flitter, barely bigger than the b-pod her brother flew for a living. Not the kind of vehicle that carried hull-piercing tools or interstellar comms.

Slowly, not letting her note waver in the slightest, she moved to step in behind the ship's captain, keeping one eye on the screen and one on the only other two people on the *Ios* who were still alive. Both were unconscious, and mercifully so. It had been killing her to listen to their thready screams.

The captain's hands clutched the edges of the console that was keeping her upright. "Attempting to hail incoming vessel."

Vessel was a polite term for what Amelie saw onscreen. The flitter looked ancient, and more beat up than her favorite pair of land boots. The kind of transport that colonies way off the beaten track held together with shoelaces and instaglue.

She closed her eyes and felt the fatigue clogging her throat. They would keep doing all the right things because Fixers didn't give up, and neither did the very tough captain of this particular small trading ship.

But shoelaces and instaglue weren't going to fix this.

-ooo-

Kish's head felt all swimmy and weird. Her DNA mother's ship had probably looked just like that.

Broken. Alone.

It was calling to her. She shook her head, trying to fix the awful pictures it was making inside her skull. It wasn't the same. This ship was new and shiny, not like the junker she'd been born on. Pops said it was a wonder that one had ever flown at all.

This one was a sleek trader ship, one of the ones that carried people and news and expensive things to colonies that could afford that kind of thing. And she could see why they'd crashed. One of the solar arms had a nasty, melted part. "They got hit by something."

Pops nodded sharply. "Space debris. People who fly out there are idiots."

Folks said the same thing about diggers. "They must have got caught in the solar storm." It had been a surprise one, or at least that's what the SatNet weather people said. No one on Halkyn VII had been surprised. Mama Simkin's big toe had been acting up again, and that always meant solar flares.

The storm had been pretty. Streaking lights in the sky. Kish looked at the ship, crashed on the side of the caldera, and felt her chin wobble. Pretty things could be mean. Every miner knew that.

She circled, eyes sharp now, looking for the flattest place she could find to set down the flitter. Not below the ship—the hills were too steep.

"No." Pops spoke sharply, moving his hands on top of hers. "Don't land—we'll hail them from here."

Her hands froze on the flitter controls as she swiveled to look at him, gaping. "We have to go help."

His eyes were angry—and full of the futile helplessness she only saw there when people were going to die. "It's a spaceship, Lakisha. They need shuttles and a rescue ship, not a couple of people in a flitter."

He never called her Lakisha. She looked down at the broken ship in horror. Halkyn VII didn't have rescue shuttles. And they were in darkside rotation—their interstellar comm couldn't send a message for hours yet.

Not a useful one, anyhow.

He laid a hand on her shoulder. "Let's hail them. Maybe we can bring them something they need. Until the rescue shuttles get here."

Pop's voice had that fake sound that happened when adults were lying about really bad things. Kish's chin wobbled some more. "I'll hold the flitter steady."

His hand on her shoulder squeezed a little.

-ooo-

Amelie winced as the crackling view screen jarred against the note she was Singing. She was tired enough now that stabilizing the interference took noticeable amounts of effort.

Butterfly wings. Just like the space junk that had clipped them and the solar flare that had knocked out their proximity detector. And the guy in engineering who had hit his head at exactly the wrong time.

The screen resolved into two blurry figures—a man

with more facial hair than Amelie had seen in cycles, and a small girl with huge blue eyes and a ghost-white face.

The Singer struggled not to react. She didn't want a child to see this.

The man's voice was brusque. "Trader ship *Ios*, what is your status?"

The captain's fingers clutched the console more tightly. "Hull breach. We've lost pressure in six of our eight sections. Five dead, two badly wounded. All of us still alive are on the bridge and trapped. One of our solar ribs was driven through the bridge doors."

Amelie had to respect that kind of capacity for understatement. There were two hundred tons of metal between them and escape. And that wasn't the worst of it.

The captain's breath rattled. "We're losing oxygen."

The man on the screen knew what that meant. Amelie could see the sad horror in his eyes and knew what *that* meant. Rescue wasn't in his power to deliver. She jerked ruthlessly on her control as her Song wobbled.

Not now. She could be weak later. If there was a later.

The captain nodded feebly at the woman behind her. "Amelie here is trying some heroics."

The man and the girl both stared, puzzled.

Amelie gulped for air in the waning oxygen supply. Earlier, she'd managed to move the solar rib enough to extract the first officer and their comms intern, for all the good it would likely do them. Now she was trying to use pure vibration to hold thousands of tiny leaks at bay.

The Singer version of shoelaces and instaglue.

The captain's head lolled to the side. Dammit, make that three survivors badly wounded. Amelie stopped singing and stepped forward. Singers weren't in the line of command on any space vessel—unless they were the only one left who could speak. "We'll need something capable of drilling a hole in the side of this ship."

The man was already shaking his head. "We have drills, but nothing big enough to get them here fast. It's going to take hours."

He sounded competent. And certain.

The little girl beside him looked ready to punch someone in the nose. "We have to help, Pops. They can disassemble the drills. We can fly the parts."

She wasn't as fragile as she looked. Amelie registered that one thought as she sucked breath to start Singing again. If she could block the leaks well enough, maybe she could buy those hours. She added volume to her note. Power. The kind of power that might save a ship.

And would almost certainly cost a Singer her life.

Amelie felt a trickle adding to hers.

Her eyes jerked to the screen. The little girl was standing now, hands fisted at her sides, face fiercely focused. Singing. Precisely matching resonance with Amelie's note.

The Singer felt her eyes bulge. Talent. Immense talent, out here in the middle of asteroid hell.

The child stiffened as her father motioned for silence. And Sang louder.

Amelie reached for the tablet in her pocket and,

sustaining the note she knew would be her last, sent off a short, seminally important message to KarmaCorp HQ. If a rescue ship ever arrived, it might even get delivered.

She looked back up into the fiery blue eyes of the child who would one day have the kind of Talent that might save this ship.

The child who didn't have enough control or knowledge to try today without putting her life on the line too. And Amelie Descol couldn't let that happen. It violated every oath she'd ever taken, every rule in KarmaCorp's very substantial manual, and every shred of human decency a dying Fixer had left.

So she shifted her gaze to the man beside the girl, looked him straight in the eyes, and let him see the truth.

He met her gaze for a long moment. And then he gave one sharp nod of respect and reached for the controls of the flitter.

The child's keening wail as the transmission ended nearly broke Amelie's heart.

And it made her smile. That one wouldn't ever back down from a fight. The child with the blue eyes would make a fine Fixer one day. The one legacy of this final horror that she could be proud of.

Today, only one Singer would die.

-ooo-

Kish couldn't see the ship anymore. They were almost back to Halkyn VII's derelict landing pad now, and the broken body of the *Ios* had disappeared from view long ago.

But she could still hear it. The woman with the green eyes, begging the stars to help.

Because the girl from the digger rock couldn't.

-ooo-

Amelie could still feel the child. Her anguish and her guilt, and the echoing resonances of a Talent that had tried to throw itself across a vacuum of space and do the impossible.

A child born to be a Fixer if she'd ever seen one.

If it please the fates, not a child destined to die as one.

Amelie took one last look around the battered bridge and then lifted her chin and blasted her high, pure note one more time out into the infinity of space. A final moment of defiance.

Then she bowed her head and changed her Song. To a lullaby. One that would send calm to the child still listening, and put everyone still alive on the ship to sleep. The gift of oblivion, as quickly as she could bring it.

Amelie felt the black coming. And Sang it welcome.

-ooo-

Three Months Later...

Pops had stopped coming with her, and when Kish got

back, he would look at her with that cross face that made his eyebrows join together and lines run up from his nose.

But her astrosuit was always charged and ready to go, every night. And even though it was battered and dinged and two sizes too big, someone had done some careful repairs on all the seams.

She had no idea why she had to be in a dumb suit out here in the cold. Singing sounded way nicer in one of the abandoned tunnels, especially if she managed to swipe her brother's heater mitts before she left. That's usually where she went to sing.

But this note—it insisted that it must be sung under the night sky.

Kish placed the carefully shaped rock that would hold the surface tube open until she returned, and stepped away from the sensors. They were rusty as hell and nobody ever bothered to look at their logs, but occasionally even beat-up old crap managed to work right, and she didn't want any more lines running up from Pop's nose.

She turned herself toward the northwest. Toward the caldera.

The broken ship wasn't there anymore. A rescue vessel had come. It had saved the captain with the sad face and the comms intern with the nice laugh and the first officer with the gruff voice and wrapped candies in his pocket.

But Kish had known they were too late for the lady with the voice of gold and the fierce, sad eyes.

She drew in a deep breath, remembering. And let the single, shattering note rise up from her ribs.

The sound reverberated inside her helmet like a space cat on synth-caf, but Kish barely noticed. She focused only on the beautiful, heartbreaking sound.

Just like always, it made tears run down her face. And just like always, her ribs felt like they might never breathe again. It had taken her two weeks to stop panicking and triple-checking the oxygen levels on her space suit.

The oxygen had always been fine.

Kish tipped her head back to the night sky and imagined her puny note rising up to the stars. She knew the stars would never hear her—she was just a girl from a digger rock, and a troublesome, skinny one at that. But she sang up to the sky anyway.

It was where the song wanted to go.

SUMMONED

YESENIA STARED at the old man on the other side of the desk. "That is not possible."

"It is almost certain." His eyes betrayed nothing. "I have verified all steps of the work myself."

She had known Regalis Marsden, Head of the Star-Readers, for almost fifteen years. In all that time, she had never known him to be wrong.

Her hand didn't move to her flat belly, but every scrap of Talent she had moved to protect what would one day grow inside her. Every scrap of her fear said it wouldn't be enough. "Death is not an acceptable outcome."

His gaze didn't waver. Regalis was a man well used to delivering news no one wanted to hear.

Normally, it was her job to listen and to figure out how to best use the resources of KarmaCorp to sway outcomes in the quadrant in the direction the Star-

Readers believed they needed to go. She respected Regalis and understood the value of his team—and why most feared them. The oracles of KarmaCorp. The elite few who stashed themselves away in an ivory tower and read the universal ether, unhampered by the messiness of human emotion and need.

The StarReaders permitted her to visit their tower more often than most. Few were capable of controlling their emotions as well as she was.

Until today.

She would not raise a hand to her belly. The discipline of that, the arbitrary line in the sand, was all that kept her from breaking. She had not known she was meant to be a mother.

Or how it would feel to know the universe planned to yank that away.

Regalis tipped his head fractionally to the left. "Do you wish to have a child?"

Yesenia swallowed her offense—many would ask the same question, and most would at least think it in tones far more unkind. "Yes." She wouldn't have imagined it, but there were no words for what had shifted inside her the moment he had asked the question.

The old man who ran the StarReaders with an iron hand watched her. Gathering his data.

She didn't flinch. He had better ability to see people as human beings than most of his kind. And he wasn't done with whatever he had summoned her here to say. She pulled enough Talent away from shielding her belly to poke his direction. StarReaders had one kind of power —she had another.

He held up a hand. "Use of Talent is not welcome in this room, Director. You're well aware of that."

She was. She also knew how many times that particular rule had been broken in the last fifteen years—she'd been present for all of them. There had been reasons, just as there were now. "I'm a Traveler, Regalis. I use Talent wherever I damn well please." That was the kind of thing she couldn't get away with saying anywhere else in the galaxy without terrifying the populace, but arrogance was expected in this room.

Respected, even.

He paused and looked off into a corner of the office, his eyes studying something far off in the distance no one else could see.

She knew every one of the tricks the man in front of her used to inspire shock and awe—and obedience. He should know her well enough by now to dispense with the StarReader smoke and mirrors. "Out with it. We both know you have something left to say, and I don't have a lot more patience."

It had taken her almost ten days to get here when his summons had arrived. She'd been out in the field monitoring the work of the newest batch of apprentice Fixers. Something her predecessor had never done, but it had been one of her top priorities right from the beginning. She'd spent the first year or two as Director getting Stardust Prime squared away, and then started the long process of mopping up the rest of the quadrant. Six years and that job wasn't nearly done, which meant she didn't have time for Regalis to play his games.

Especially when there was a threat to what was hers.

She would not touch her belly, even if death stalked what would one day grow there. Regalis had been very clear. The forces that would come were terrible ones. A threat not yet visible, not yet felt, not yet conceived—but seen in the stars. Regalis could not see the nature of the darkness, simply that it would come. And that it would bring with it annihilation.

He turned his head back to hers. "We both know I owe you a favor, Yesenia."

He did. Of the largest possible dimensions. It terrified her that he referred to it now. She let not a molecule of that fear show on her face.

His pause this time wasn't smoke and mirrors—it was something she'd never seen before in this room, in this tower, on this planet.

A StarReader caught in a moment of uncertainty.

Regalis Marsden, grappling with doubt.

Yesenia had visited eight timelines with skills most of the universe—past, present, and future—thought were impossible. She'd righted unthinkable wrongs, gently adjusted entire eras, ridden majestically into assignments so vast she couldn't begin to comprehend their importance—all at the behest of the man in front of her.

Not once had he ever hesitated.

"There is one possible alternative." His eyes were opaque. "If you do this, if you even consider it, you must leave the threads of time undisturbed. It is imperative."

The dread deepened. That wasn't something he would say without very specific ideas of what she must do —and not do. "I'm listening." She would make no promises—and she understood that she had made them anyhow simply by continuing to stand in this room.

He bowed his head slightly. "The stars allow for one small, difficult possibility."

She listened as one of the oldest and hardest men in the galaxy laid out a plan that would use every mote of her Talent and every nanogram of her will. A birth buried in the sands of time. A hundred perilous adjustments to hold that act of flagrant disobedience out of history and memory and the energetic imprint of the universe.

A task that the most prodigious Talent ever to grace KarmaCorp's hallowed halls knew went far beyond what she should even attempt. But it would give her a chance, albeit a tiny one, to keep at least part of the sacred promise she had already made to what would one day grow inside her.

The alternative was death.

Her hands went to her belly. It no longer mattered what Regalis saw.

His eyes darkened. "You *must* leave the threads of time undisturbed, Yesenia."

She would not let the tears fall. She would not. "I will do it exactly as you have said, but I *will* do it. I will bring her back." No matter what it cost her as a mother.

He nodded, very slowly. "I have not said all. Listen to me now, and listen well."

Nothing in her wanted to keep listening—but she would not risk her daughter's life because she was weak.

Regalis Marsden's eyes were hard, black marbles. "If you save her, they must not know that she is important to you."

Her hands clutched at her belly, and somewhere deep inside, a warrior she had not even known existed rose in maternal rage. "That is not possible. She's my daughter."

"It is not her lineage that will matter. It is whether or not she makes you vulnerable. If they can trace a crack from her to you, your efforts will have been entirely in vain." If there had ever been humanity in his eyes, it wasn't there any longer. "The stars are clear. It is either that, or death. You may choose."

Death allowed by StarReader edict. She knew that as well as she knew her own name. Regalis would never permit a child, even hers, to threaten the existence of all that they knew.

He turned his chair to look out the window, his voice as remote as if they'd never met. "The threads of time must remain undisturbed."

She took a deep, strained breath, trying to keep a leash on her wild need to leap across the desk and strangle him where he sat. Regalis had an ego the size of a galaxy cluster, but he had also just entrusted her with knowledge that empowered her to blast the galaxy as they knew it into smithereens.

Even in her fury, she understood the magnitude of that gift. With anyone else, the Head of the StarReaders would have dismissed the infinitesimally small possibility of threading a needle through time and risk and terrible odds and leaving the universe intact.

No one else would have been given a choice.

Regalis Marsden, paying off his debt.

TADPOLE SCHOOL

HER FAVORITE TIME OF YEAR—AND the one she most dreaded.

Lucinda Coffey, or Bean to everyone on Stardust Prime, looked around the small meadow where she'd chosen to host the welcome reception for the incoming first-year trainees. She'd appreciate the view and the sunny warmth and the buzz of excitement later. Right now, she was looking for trouble.

There always was some. No class of tadpoles ever landed entirely easily, and she was already quite certain this one wasn't going to be an exception.

There was just no way to uproot two dozen ten-year-olds from everything they'd ever known without some bumps. And that was maybe as it should be. Yanking around people's lives wasn't a responsibility she ever wanted to take lightly, and it had been her fingers doing much of the yanking for most of the children here. The world might blame Yesenia Mayes, or the vast organization behind her, but Bean knew better.

For these kids, the buck stopped at her desk.

"Stop fretting." The Director's shadow suddenly materialized beside her. "You haven't lost one yet."

That was as close as Yesenia ever came to empathy. "There's always a first time." And if this was it, it would happen with the fierce blonde child currently trying to murder everything with her eyes.

Bean sighed. She'd hoped that sunshine and ice cream would at least make a dent there. Maybe it was time to send Danelle over. The friendly Dancer was one of their best at helping tadpoles to settle, and young enough to remember her own arrival at trainee school more clearly than most. Maybe she could help defuse the bomb of fear that was Lakisha Drinkwater.

Bean knew that most people wouldn't read the young girl's body language as fear. The child was smart and had obviously spent more than a few hours in dark mining tunnels facing down threats bigger than she was. But underneath the layers of pugnacious fury rode a child who was terrified right down to her molecules.

Something Lucinda Coffey knew because she, too, had spent some time in dark tunnels—and had eventually been dragged out of them.

She had not thanked the people who had done the dragging.

Yesenia followed Bean's gaze. "That's the child Amelie Descol found?"

The Singer who had died two years ago in one of the

bigger screw-ups of KarmaCorp's history. Bean's fingers hadn't been on those reins, at least not directly, but she had felt the reverberations. "Yes."

"She's got enough attitude for six."

Bean knew the woman beside her well enough to hear beyond the official tone of disapproval. "I imagine she'll be in your office a time or two." Standing on the wildly colorful rug that gave lie to everything Yesenia Mayes insisted the world believe about who she was. It always astonished Bean that she was the only person on Stardust Prime who seemed to find that rug significant.

People had eyes, but they didn't generally use them.

Yesenia, on the other hand, could see things that ordinary assistants couldn't. Bean nodded her chin at their young blonde trainee and pitched her voice low enough to keep it out of passing ears. "Think I should send Danelle in?"

"No." The answer came instantly, followed by a pause as the Director took a second look.

Bean held still as the air shifted in the strange way it did when the boss lady was using her unique blend of Talents. There was more than one reason people trembled on her rug.

"No." The same answer, but with more depth this time—and some unexpected notes of surprise. "The energies are moving around her in interesting ways. Let them work."

Bean pursed her lips. Yesenia's job was to use Karma-Corp's Talents in pursuit of universal good. That didn't always translate into doing the best thing for individual ten-year-old girls.

That was the job of assistants.

"The Director is right," said a voice behind them both. "Help comes for the child. She calls in what she needs. She has much power, that one."

Those were the kinds of mystical words that Karma-Corp very much tried to avoid. Talents were science, or at least it made people much more comfortable when that was the official party line. Bean wasn't at all sure the party line was right, but she knew better than to spout anything different. The regal, elderly woman who had joined them was a different matter entirely, however. Mundi was clan matriarch of the Lightbodies, the family who grew all the food on Stardust Prime and had a finger in pretty much everything else on the planet, too. Bean smiled—Mundi was one of her favorite people on-planet or off, and if she was on the job, Lakisha Drinkwater was in excellent hands. "I'll hold off on Danelle, then."

Mundi inclined her head, acknowledging the deftly delivered compliment. "The girl needs her first drink of root water. It comes."

Yesenia scowled. "You see things, old woman. Someone should have tested you for Talent long ago."

The woman who ran the Lightbody clan with an iron fist only snorted. "Many have tried, including the previous tenant in your job, Director. I'm only an old woman, nothing more."

One with a particular interest in this group of

tadpoles. Bean looked around, scanning the group for Mundi's great-granddaughter.

"She's over by the food." Mundi seemed amused.

Bean knew exactly how much pull a certain clan had on Stardust Prime, and food was one of their primary currencies. She was very glad they were on her side. "Thank you for providing such a lovely welcome buffet." The food was truly wondrous—plump berries and fresh breads, and even some homemade ice cream.

"It is our pleasure." The old woman sounded as if she truly meant it. "The transplanting is difficult for these young ones, even those who were eager to come. Fertile soil will help them thrive."

The Lightbodies knew everything there was to know about good dirt. "I've seen more than one kid licking strawberry juice off their fingers." Which on most inner-planet worlds was enough of a breach of manners for the average ten-year-old to refrain from doing it unless the temptation level ran awfully high.

Bean hoped there were some strawberries left at the end so she could throw manners to the wind too.

Mundi smiled and patted her arm. "There's a bowl of them on your desk. A reward for a job well done."

A reward, and a message. The Lightbodies would be watching this particular group of tadpoles closely. That didn't upset Bean at all. The energies of the universe sometimes leaned hard on trainees long before they were ready. A wall of tough gardeners standing in the way was a gift to every child on this field, even if it might some-times make KarmaCorp business more difficult.

Mundi winked, and then patted Yesenia's arm as well. "I believe my grandson dropped off some strawberries for you too."

Bean hid a grin—if the boss lady had a weakness, garden-ripened fruit was absolutely it. Something Mundi knew and wielded ferociously when the occasion demanded it.

Yesenia nodded her head graciously at Mundi. "Thank you." She waved a hand in the general direction of the milling trainees. "I believe I'll go circulate again and make sure all the new arrivals know who I am."

Mundi, who might just have the best poker face in the galaxy, smiled slightly. "It's always good to begin as you mean to go on."

Yesenia's left cheek twitched slightly. "Exactly." She gave a last nod and walked off slowly, eyes on the meadow, a general planning her strategy, surveying her troops.

"Come." Mundi's hand was on Bean's shoulder. "Let's go see if there are any tasty nibbles left to be had."

It was entirely tempting, but she wanted to keep an eye on ticking bombs and other worrisome elements. "I'll stay here, thank you."

"You'll come." This time, the words brooked no argument. "The energies are moving more strongly around your fierce young charge. The view for what is coming will be better from there."

Bean blinked, and then stuck her hand in Mundi's elbow. She knew better than to argue with an old woman who saw things.

Especially when there were unhappy ten-year-olds involved.

-ooo-

There were trees. Big, horrifying skeletons with green, flapping bits of skin, just like in the horror vids she watched at Jingo's when Mom and Pops weren't paying attention. School showed the dumb nature vids where the trees were nice and friendly and people liked to climb their skeletons, but no kid from a digger rock believed that stuff.

Kish looked around for someplace to hide. If the trees started rampaging and eating people, she didn't want to be the first one to die. She was going back to Halkyn VII as fast as she could figure out how to get there, and she didn't plan to arrive as a little container of ashes.

The trees were spread out randomly in an area bigger than any room she'd ever seen, and the carpet was spiky green stuff she was pretty sure was grass. Every so often, the carpet would have a hole and colorful flowers poked up, reminding everyone that they were walking on dirt.

She shivered and tried to tell herself that dirt wasn't all that different from rock dust. Except for the billions of microbes and other tiny little monsters they'd learned about in science class.

This dirt could eat you.

There wasn't a decent hiding spot anywhere that she could see. She should have packed her drill—this planet needed some tunnels, and it wouldn't take her long to make one big enough to tuck away in. Pops had always said she was too damn small to make a decent miner. That was probably why he'd agreed to send her off on this crazy trip.

Not that the KarmaCorp people had given anyone much choice. They'd just kept talking about how special her singing was, and Federation laws, and the Very Bad Things that would happen if she didn't leave with them. Plus they'd promised that she'd get a really good education, better than anyone on Halkyn VII had probably ever seen. Which hadn't impressed Kish any, but it had swayed Mom and Pops.

They hadn't looked too sad when she left. They were used to losing kids, except it was usually a mining tunnel that ate them.

Maybe if she got eaten by a really big tree, they'd feel bad for making her come.

Kish scrunched sideways, trying to hide in the shadows of the one small piece of polymer wall she'd found. Her eyes relaxed in the relative darkness. This planet was way too bright—someone needed to dial down the fake sunshine a whole bunch.

Her shoulders shifted inside the strange new skin-suit the Seeker lady had made her wear on the shuttle. The one that said she was a KarmaCorp trainee, right on the pocket underneath her name. As soon as she could find a needle, she was picking out most of the letters. Nobody called her Lakisha unless they were really mad.

Then again, she was pretty good at making people get

that way, so maybe she should just leave the fancy red letters the way they were.

Kish took a careful breath. The air here smelled weird, full of tree breath and slimy things. Her science teacher said tree breath was good for them, but she preferred her air full of rock dust and the smell of sweaty socks. Only inner-planet wimps needed their air all clean and pretty.

She looked around in disgust. Probably all the students here were from inner planets. Most of them didn't even look smart enough to be scared of the trees.

One of the greeter people who were trying to make them all feel welcome glanced her way, and then frowned and headed over. Kish stood her ground, even though her legs were shaking. If you ran, the trees could see you easier.

"Hello, sweetheart." The lady with the green eyes and the weird hair flashed a totally fake smile. "Why don't you come and meet some of the other trainees? I'm sure you'll feel much better if you make some new friends."

Kish tried to drill a hole through the lady's face with the power of her eyes. "I feel just fine."

Green eyes blinked really fast. "I'm sure you do, dear. Would you like something to eat? There are some fresh strawberries from the garden—if you've never had those, they're a real treat."

They ate things that grew in the dirt. Kish shuddered. If Mom and Pops knew that, maybe they wouldn't have made her come.

"You're a Singer, aren't you?" The welcome lady was looking a little sickly now. "I hear you have a beautiful voice. You'll be a great asset to KarmaCorp and the important work we do in the galaxy."

She didn't want to sing. She wanted to be a driller—or maybe a pilot, if she could talk her way into showing someone with a flitter how well she could fly. It was okay to be small if you were a pilot, and her hands were the best. Even Pops said so.

Kish kept sliding her feet slowly away, hoping the annoying lady would get the hint and go try to feed someone else dirt food. She still had some ration bars in her bag—she'd eat those when she got back to her room.

Her really big, really bright room. With a window that the trees could see in when they came to snatch her in the night.

She looked around, desperate for a corner or some shadows or even a decent-sized rock.

"Those are weird boots."

Kish spun around, fists already up. This might be an alien planet full of scary things she didn't know how to deal with, but she knew exactly what a bully sounded like and how to deal with one. When you were small, it was important to land the first punch—and to make it a good one.

She had good hands for that, too.

The kid behind her took one look at her fists and fled.

Kish watched her run and kept the sneer off her face. Inner-planet wimp.

"Are you hungry? My dad says that when my baby

cousins are in a bad mood, they probably need to eat or sleep."

Kish turned toward the new voice and kept her fists up.

This arrival didn't look as easy to scare as the last one. Her brown eyes gazed calmly out of a friendly face covered in drawings that looked a little bit like some of the flowers, only less scary. Her hair was done up in some fancy rolls that belonged on a vid star or a queen, but her hands had some kind of dust on them. The name on her skinsuit said Tyra Lightbody.

The girl glanced down at her chest. "Oh, that. Nobody calls me Tyra. I'm Tee." She held up her palm in the way the inner planets used to greet each other. "Nice to meet you. Want half my sandwich?" She held out the plate in her other hand.

Kish almost reached for it before she saw the contents. The bread looked almost normal, but there was green stuff in the sandwich. And something red and shiny and the color of blood. She stuffed her hands behind her back. "No, thanks."

Tee looked at her sandwich with confusion. "It's really good, and I can tell that you're hungry—your belly is being really loud."

As if on cue, Kish's stomach let out another rumble. She swallowed and backed away. "I mostly eat ration bars." At least those didn't grow in the dirt.

"Oh." Comprehension dawned on the other girl's face. "You must come from somewhere that doesn't grow their own food, right?" She nodded over her shoulder.

"Come on—there's some stuff on the table that we brought specially for people like you until you get used to eating real food."

Kish could feel herself trying to get mad at the words, but that funny feeling in her belly that always seemed to know true things wasn't listening to the words. It was looking into friendly brown eyes and seeing something important there. Tyra Lightbody might look funny with her fancy hair and the drawings on her face, but she sounded kind. And she knew where the special food was. Kish gulped and swallowed down her pride. "Can we not walk too close to the trees? Please?"

Tee's eyes opened really wide—and then something shifted and she just nodded and reached for Kish's hand. "Sure. Do people call you Lakisha or something different?"

Kish blinked as she felt herself hauled away from the wall and onto the carpet of grass. Tee's hand was warm, like a drill that had been running for a couple of hours. Kish had the strangest sense that the warmth was telling her not to worry, that everything would be fine.

And the even stranger sense that she maybe wanted to believe it.

-oOo-

Tee grinned as she dragged her new friend toward the buffet table. Somehow she always found the weird ones. That was okay—Mundi said that weird people made the most interesting friends.

And Kish needed a friend, just like she needed the calm that Tee was pushing out of her hand. It was something she'd just learned to do, to take a plant's energy and pass it to someone. It only worked when she was touching them, but still, it was pretty cool.

Right now, she was sending Kish some energy from the sleepy patch of bluebells she'd helped her little cousin water right before the welcome picnic started. She wouldn't tell Kish that yet. If she was scared of tomatoes, she probably didn't want to hear about bluebells, either. That could wait until after they'd been friends for a few more days. It was important to be honest with people you liked, but maybe not right away this time. Mundi said there were exceptions to every rule, and growing up was about learning when to make them.

Tee didn't really want to grow up—it sounded complicated.

As they got closer to the buffet table, she steered them toward the end with all the processed foods. It hurt her Lightbody heart to see it there next to the real stuff, but she supposed if you grew up eating stuff that came from a machine, that was what you would want if you were feeling all messed up inside.

Kish might look angry on the outside, but her insides were mostly scared and lonely and confused.

Tee slid into an empty spot at the edge of the table and picked up a plate. "What looks good?"

Her new friend stared. "Um, some of the potatoes, maybe? And if there's some hamburger?"

Tee couldn't let anyone she liked eat nasty machine

meat, but the stuff that was supposed to be mashed potatoes didn't look too bad. She took a big spoonful and dropped it on Kish's plate.

"Me too, please." A plate reached between their shoulders, attached to a bubbly voice and the wildest red hair Tee had ever seen.

The new girl grinned at both of them and pulled another trainee up beside her. "Hi. I'm Iggy, and this is Raven." She reached for a spoon and helped herself to something that might be fake carrots. "I know some of you are all excited about the real food, but I'm a spoiled brat from an inner planet, and I'm kind of freaked out about stuff that grows in the dirt."

She was telling the truth—kind of. With their arms touching, Tee could feel Iggy's fondness for the fake carrots, but she could also feel her interest and kindness as she plopped some of the carrots on Kish's plate. Helping the kid from the digger rock feel less strange.

Tee decided instantly that she liked Iggy.

Raven stood behind them all, not saying much and watching everything, but when Tee looked at her, she smiled. "I eat real food, but I'm full."

There was kindness there, too—and something that felt a little bit like what lived inside Mundi. Something old and wise and tough and really, really smart. Tee tucked that tidbit away. Raven was going to make a really good grown-up.

And probably the auntie of this new little tribe. Tee could feel the rightness of it, the connecting of the four of them, even if not everybody in the group had figured it out just yet.

Kish especially. Her face was calmer now, but her hand in Tee's was still spewing energy that felt a little bit like when Tinker the cat had fallen into Aunt Minia's pond.

Tee just smiled and kept holding on while Iggy filled plates and Raven stood witness. She knew what Kish needed. In two days it would be Sunday, and she would bring her new friend to the Lightbody family dinner. It would be outside in the courtyard at this time of year, and full of laughter and fun and enough food that her new friend would never have to be scared of an empty belly ever again.

And the aunties would make sure she tried the real stuff.

Tee looked over at the other two, Iggy and Raven, trying out their names on the tongue of her heart. They would be friends too, and good ones. The dirt under her feet liked them, and that was all the votes she needed. She'd bring them to Sunday dinner too—just not the first one. They would love the Lightbodies, but Kish *needed* them.

Always heal the plants with the most damage first.

It made Tee sad that KarmaCorp had done this thing. There had to be a way to collect the tadpoles without hurting so many of them. Kish wasn't the only sad face today, or the only scared heart. She was just the angriest —and judging by the looks the teachers were casting their way, they all knew it too.

Tee didn't say anything, she just stood firm and let them look. There was a Lightbody on the job now.

"You live here?" Raven had started them moving, even though it didn't look like she was doing anything. Just like the aunties.

"Yeah." Tee hadn't figured out yet whether the other trainees would think that was a good thing or a bad thing. "My family grows the food for Stardust Prime."

"Cool." Iggy's eyes were alight with interest, flitting from the conversation to the goings-on around them and back again. "That must mean you know where to find all the good stuff."

"Probably." It wasn't bragging to tell the truth. "What kind of stuff do you want to find?"

"A tunnel." Kish looked shocked to hear the sound of her own voice and quickly ducked her head. "Never mind."

Tee knew better than to ignore anything said with that much wishing energy behind it. Stardust Prime didn't run to very many underground passageways, but it had a lot of other cool things. She tried to think about why somebody from a mining planet might want a tunnel. "Do you want to know where the shortcuts are, or someplace away from trees, or good hiding spots?"

"Yes. All of those." Iggy wrapped an arm around Kish's shoulders. "Well, I'm okay with trees, but shortcuts and hidey holes are both good things."

Kish looked about as comfortable as a frog in a space-suit, but Tee was pretty sure Iggy knew that. She watched Iggy's fingers fluttering, and wondered. A

Dancer, probably. She walked like one, and most Dancers couldn't hold still for very long.

She side-eyed Raven as the girl with dark hair and dark eyes guided them into a cluster of rocks. "Singer, Dancer, Grower—you must be the Shaman." One of each of the Talents. It had a nice kind of balance to it.

"So they tell me." Raven took a seat at the foot of a small boulder and watched as Iggy delivered Kish to the biggest of the rocks.

Tee smiled as Kish plopped right down on its flat top and exhaled like she'd finally found friendly dirt.

"Eat." Iggy stuffed a big spoon in Kish's hand and then dropped gracefully into a cross-legged seat on the ground, eyeing her own plate with obvious hunger.

Tee sat last, closest to the grove of trees, and took off her shoes. Feeding energy into rocks was a little harder than talking to the plants, but not much. Rocks were just dirt that hadn't happened yet. She reached deep for some of the good, rooted sense of home that lived under her toes and channeled it, letting it gently touch the rock of her new friend with the blonde hair and the hungry belly and the ferocious eyes.

And jumped as a new vibration came through the dirt.

She opened her eyes, not realizing she'd closed them, and saw bare brown toes next to her own. Raven didn't say anything. She just reached for Tee's hand and gathered both their energies and tied them together somehow.

Tee had never felt Shaman energy before, and she had no idea what Raven had done, but she could see the result. More than rooting and home was flowing into the rock now. Wisps of story. Reassurance. Grandfather spirits.

She blinked. Raven was totally like Mundi, only stronger.

Iggy looked their direction and winked, one hand shoveling in spoonfuls of fake carrot, the other rippling in tiny motions over the ground.

Tee didn't know what the Dancer was doing either, but she didn't need to know. The important part was right in front of her eyes.

Kish was eating, and her eyes didn't look so mad anymore.

And the rest of them had just done their first job as Fixers.

-ooo-

The carrots were good, the threads in the meadow had stopped looking quite so frazzled, and she had new friends with some pretty cool tricks. Iggy scraped up the last bite of carrots on her plate and grinned. Not bad for her first day.

And nobody had said anything about the huge pile of mashed potatoes on her plate or the fact that her fingers could never stop moving.

Madame Tsarnova would have lectured her five times by now on the importance of a dancer controlling all her motions and on watching every bite of what she put in her mouth. Iggy had never taken that part seriously—

she'd been born a stick and was pretty sure she was going to stay that way no matter how many mashed potatoes she ate. But dancer discipline had been part of every breath at the Tsarnova School of Dance.

Or it had been until the day the woman with pretty brown eyes and the no-nonsense voice had shown up and told Madame Tsarnova that she would be losing three of her best students. Iggy first, and then Cassie and Adoba would come next year. They were all going to be the KarmaCorp kind of Dancers now.

The woman with the pretty brown eyes had moved her fingers a lot too.

Iggy did it because it helped her see the tiny threads of energy that ran everywhere, and to move them where they needed to be. Dancing was the best way to move them, but in the last couple of rotations, she'd figured out how to do it while she was sitting mostly still, too.

Iggy glanced behind her, using the dancer trick of watching without anyone really knowing you were look-ing. Kish was almost done with her food, and she looked more relaxed now—or at least, not ready to leap up and chop everyone in the meadow into little pieces.

Even Madame Tsarnova's eyes hadn't been that tough.

Maybe they would all grow up to have tough eyes. The lady who ran KarmaCorp here had the seriously scary kind. Iggy glanced around, looking for where the threads got really dense. Yesenia Mayes had more threads attached to her than Iggy had ever seen.

Iggy found the Director, and saw a couple of the

thickest threads brighten. "Something's about to happen."

Raven and Tee swiveled to look the direction she was pointing.

A small woman with her hair done up in short braids and beads stepped into their line of view and held up her hands. "Hi, everyone. I'm Bean, but I'm pretty sure you all know that already. Welcome to Stardust Prime, and if you didn't get any strawberries yet, you should come see me in a few minutes and I'll make sure you get hooked up, okay?"

Several students licked their fingers and grinned.

Iggy wasn't going to leave Kish as the only trainee who didn't eat strawberries, but she hoped her new friend caved once she saw them. Strawberries were pretty much the best thing ever, even if they did grow in dirt.

Bean was moving her hands again in the way that said she wasn't a Dancer, but she was a really nice person. "We're going to have a couple of people talk for a few minutes, but they promised they wouldn't be boring. Danelle Oscara is one of your teachers, and she'll say a little bit about what will happen at school tomorrow morning."

"Is it true they call us tadpoles?"

Iggy couldn't see the face of whoever had called out, but she liked the sound of their voice.

"Absolutely." Bean grinned. "Does anyone know what a tadpole is?"

"Yeah," said the same voice with disgust. "It's a little

baby fish that's going to turn into a frog one day, but all they are at first is a tiny brain and a tail."

Bean looked like she was going to laugh any minute. "Ever try to catch one?"

Silence, and then heads shook all over the field as trainees checked in with their neighbors.

The woman with the beads in her hair nodded, still smiling. "I figure that all those people who say tadpoles have tiny brains are just mad at being outwitted by something so small. People underestimate tadpoles, it's true." She lowered her voice to a stage whisper. "Your job, every year, is to remind them how silly that is."

Iggy grinned as half the threads on the meadow shimmered brighter. Trainees, all a little happier to be here.

Even the energy behind her shimmied a little. Kish might not look like she was listening, but she was.

"Before Danelle talks to you, though," Bean drew their attention back her way, "Director Mayes is here, and she wanted a chance to welcome you."

The threads in the meadow wobbled as Bean stepped to the side and the stern lady with the black hair and eyes even tougher than Madame Tsarnova stepped forward. Iggy thought she moved like a Dancer, but the Google-Plex said she was more than that. A Traveler—a Fixer with all the Talents. Iggy was really glad she only had one. The stories about Travelers had been awfully sad.

The Director looked around at all the faces, her eyes pausing briefly on each one. Iggy tried not to flinch as the four of them on the rocks got surveyed, but she couldn't stop her fingers from wiggling just a little.

Her heart nearly stopped when the stern lady's fingers wiggled back.

Iggy froze—it wasn't trouble. More like a welcome. And something else that might almost be pleasure.

She felt the red rising in her cheeks. She hadn't meant to call attention to herself.

And then Iggy felt steadiness at her back. A long, low tone of it, almost like the rock behind her was humming. She thought maybe she was imagining it, but then the Director's eyes widened and she knew it was real.

Iggy leaned back, listening to the quiet music of the rock—and then realized it wasn't the rock singing. It was Kish. A tough-as-nails, reliable-as-ancient-hunks-of-granite message in a single note.

She had a friend at her back.

Iggy felt her hands fluttering, and the deep need in her body to jump up and send relief-happiness-joy out into the universe. But she also knew, as surely as night turned into morning, that if she did that, the girl behind her would go find one of those tunnels and never come out ever again.

So she sat as still as she possibly could and only let her fingers move.

She figured Kish couldn't see the tears on her cheeks, so those were okay too.

"Some of you already know why you're here." Director Mayes was looking right square at the four of them as she started speaking, and then she let her gaze travel again. "And some of you might not figure it out for a rotation or two."

Nobody said a word, but Iggy could see the confusion on the field. They all knew why they were here—to be Fixers.

"Most of you come from worlds where you have a vague idea that you'd like to do good things in the universe." Yesenia Mayes paused a moment, letting the energy in the threads build. "Here, it is expected of you. You're part of KarmaCorp now, and we are a force for good in the galaxy. You will spend the next ten years learning how you will be part of that, discovering your own strengths and weaknesses and how to get the job done in spite of both."

Iggy wasn't sure she understood what that meant, but she was mesmerized anyhow.

"At some point in the next few months, every single one of you will want to leave." The Director's eyes were as harsh as her words. "Some of you will be in my office when it happens, and some of you will be crying on Bean's lap."

The woman with the beads in her hair didn't look at all discomfited by that idea, but everyone else did.

"You will not leave." Yesenia's words were blunt, and Iggy felt Kish tensing behind her. "You belong here, even on the days when it feels like that might not be true. You have great gifts, and the people and the worlds in this quadrant need your help. One day, if you work hard enough and apply yourselves with enough discipline and fortitude, you just might be good enough to actually help them."

Her eyes scanned the absolute silence of the meadow.

"For now, you are tadpoles. Your job is to swim fast and learn quickly and transform into what the universe needs you to become. There are many here who will help you with that job. Be smart and let them. Those of you who can't manage that will see me in my office, and I can promise you that neither of us will enjoy that overly much. Welcome to KarmaCorp."

Iggy blinked. Her insides were quivering like jelly. Even Raven looked a little shaken, and Tee's eyes might be clear, but her fingers clutched handfuls of dirt.

Threads all over the meadow spoke of fear and awe and trembling.

Except for one.

The one running to the girl on the rock behind her, holding a plate that had once held carrots and potatoes.

That thread was laughing.

-ooo-

Phew. The boss lady was tough.

And somehow that had made Kish feel better. Raven could feel the energies up on the flat rock calming, finding their groove.

Kish understood tough.

She wasn't alone in that. The grandmothers on Raven's home world had guardian spirits of rock and eagle, bear and wild ocean waves.

But this was a different kind of tough. Raven looked back at the woman Tee had called the boss lady. Yesenia Mayes looked fierce right down to her shiny black footwear, but something around her shimmered. Back home, they would have called it her spirit web, but Aurie said that KarmaCorp people didn't use words like that. She said they were good people, but still trying too hard to understand things that the People had always known were true.

Raven knew she could have stayed home. Karma-Corp believed they found all the people who could move the energies in special ways, but she knew it wasn't true. The People had kept more than one safe in their midst—and kept alive more ways of knowing the world than any corporation could ever understand. But Aurie had left when KarmaCorp had come for her, and when Raven had begun manifesting her gifts, Grandmother had sent for Aurie and they had taken Raven deep into the woods and up one of the highest mountains and given her the choice.

She had known she was meant to come, just like Aurie and so many others before her.

The People were a rich source of Talent.

Aurie said they would call her a Shaman here, and not to be shocked. That word didn't mean what it did to the People—it described her gift, nothing more.

Still, it was a word she associated with wisdom and leadership and long years, not a word for a girl, even one who felt things and saw things that many others didn't. That was merely an accident of birth. What she did with it would be what mattered—whether she honored what she had been given.

She had chosen to honor like Aurie did—by working

with KarmaCorp. By serving the greater good on worlds far beyond her own so that one day, she could return to the People and soak in the wisdom of the grandmothers and know that she had done well.

Raven looked at Yesenia Mayes one more time. She could feel the squeaky feeling that sometimes happened in her head when a message from the spirit grandmothers wanted to get out. Maybe the boss lady understood about spirits, but if she did, she wasn't wearing any of the usual clues, and something about this planet kept reminding Raven to keep those words inside.

Even if the Director's belly already wore a spirit web that was fierce and strong for a child that had not yet been conceived.

Raven sent a gentle pulse toward the babe that would be. *I see you.*

The spirit web wrapped around the boss lady's belly bobbed a little. Message received.

A small sound came from beside her as red hair and bright eyes moved in a little closer. Iggy was watching Raven's face, her fingers still moving, even though the rest of her was settling into stillness. "You're one of the quiet thinkers, huh?"

"No." Raven grinned. Iggy's spirit web was awesome, and it said they were going to be fast, fierce friends. "I just wait until I have something important to say."

"Not me. I say whatever comes out of my mouth. Mostly I get distracted, though. Mama says I have the focus of a hyperactive grasshopper."

Grasshoppers weren't something Raven had ever

seen, but she knew about animal medicine. And she had the oddest feeling nobody had ever taken Iggy seriously enough. Which was foolish, because the Dancer's spirit web spoke of flitting and flying, but it also spoke of strength and complexity and a soul that could see all the things.

Maybe that was why Iggy's fingers moved so much. "You're going to be a really important Dancer." Raven froze when she realized she'd spoken out loud. Aurie had warned her about that too, about saying things as if she knew they were true. She said it could spook people.

Red curls tilted almost sideways. "Cool. How do you know?"

Apparently, Iggy didn't spook too easily. That was a good thing in a best friend. "I just know stuff sometimes."

"That's what Shamans do." Tee had joined them, and she leaned in, putting an arm around each of their shoulders.

Raven looked around behind her. Kish was still sitting on the boulder, her arms around her knees, looking like she would kill the first person who got any closer. Probably because some of the trainees were milling around now and threatening to do just that.

Iggy made a soft, sympathetic sound. "She still looks really scared."

Kish looked about as scared as a hungry rattlesnake. Even her spirit web was mad.

"She's a long way from home." Tee's voice was quiet, and it sounded very grown up. "She doesn't know much about KarmaCorp or anything, and I think the grass and the trees and the flowers are making her nervous."

More sounds of sympathy from Iggy, along with some beautiful hand flourishes. "I get it. This place does feel kind of wild."

Raven looked up into the bubble-sustained atmosphere of Stardust Prime and around at the manicured meadow, confused. This was nothing like the jungle canopies and wild undergrowth of home.

"We all come from something different." Tee smiled, nestling her head on Iggy's shoulder. "You grew up in an inner world, so I bet you've hardly seen a tree except for a tiny park you went to for special field trips."

Iggy grimaced and nodded. "Something like that."

Raven could see the lines of wisdom now. "And I'm from a wild world." That wasn't what the People called it, but she'd heard foreigners use the nickname often enough.

"Right." Tee circled her palms in a symmetrical encompassing of everything around her. "I've always lived with this, so it feels totally right and normal for me."

It was part of the peace in Tee's spirit web—she was deeply connected to this place. But also in her web were the strands that said that someday the girl with the flowers drawn on her face would have to separate from what she knew and loved or her soul would be forever small. Her walk might look easier today, but it wouldn't stay that way.

None of them had easy walks. Raven looked over at

Kish, still guarding her boulder. "Does anyone know what a mining world is like?"

Iggy nodded slowly. "I have a cousin who did a rotation on one. He said it was just a big rock and black sky and lots of dark and mud and cold."

It was hard to imagine how spirits could grow in such a place. "Is that why she's so angry? Because she's never been warm or seen trees or anything?"

"I don't think so." Tee shook her head, and her voice was back to sounding really grown up. "My dad says that even when a plant grows in hard dirt, it learns to be happy there, and anything else will feel difficult and strange."

It was more than that, and now that Raven was paying attention, she could see it as clearly as if Kish had a message tattooed on her forehead. "She didn't want to come."

Iggy's eyes opened wider. "But she's going to be a KarmaCorp Fixer."

"You're from an inner world. KarmaCorp is respected there." Raven knew what it was to be from a world that didn't revere anything from the outside—but like Iggy and Tee, she wanted to be here, had chosen to put her feet on this path, and had done it with the support and love of her entire family.

Kish's spirit web wasn't just angry. It was torn. Uprooted. Raven didn't have words for what she could see, but she could feel the bright, shining truth of it now that she was looking right. And she already knew that she wasn't the best of them at working with wisdom lines.

Carefully, mindful of Aurie's words about how Karma-Corp did things differently, Raven balled up the end of the line she could see and tossed it to her new Dancer friend.

Quick fingers caught it deftly. "Oh." Iggy shaped the thread, did things with it that would have tangled Raven's brain for ten cycles. "Oh. I can see."

"See what?" Tee practically shoved her head between Iggy's dancing hands. "I don't see anything."

Raven tried to remember what Aurie had said about Growers. Touch. They worked through touch. She reached forward and grabbed Tee's hand, motioning for Iggy to do the same.

Understanding lit between the three of them, hot and bright and good. It wasn't the same as walking the webs with Grandmother and Aurie, but it wasn't so very different, either. Raven's heart rejoiced. She had made the right choice.

Now they just had to help a friend make hers.

Carefully, remembering that she worked with those not of the People, Raven pushed intention down both her hands. Iggy's feet moved faster as the energy landed, and the light inside Tee glowed brighter.

Shimmering with new understanding, the three of them shifted as a unit and went to collect their friend. Kish might not know where she belonged yet—but they did.

They were the four.

A CHILD IS BORN

BEAN WALKED into the podcare nursery, breathing out the annoyances of her day. Three trainee Fixers accidentally left behind on the strip at Vegas Station was a minor annoyance, nothing more. She'd dispatched a crew to pick them up, pronto—and sternly worded messages from Director Yesenia Mayes to everyone of any rank higher than a compost collector on Vegas.

Standard assistant protocols, except for the part where Director Mayes had been unaccountably absent from her desk for the last three days.

Now it was time to cuddle some babies.

She'd been coming twice a week for over five years, and it still hadn't gotten old, even if it had started kind of strangely. Just a short, handwritten note left on her desk one day, suggesting that the nursery could use some volunteers—the kind of note that had started Bean's old greaser instincts humming almost six years after she'd laid them officially to rest. Yesenia didn't handwrite notes, and she never told Bean what to do in her spare time, not without it having a greater purpose, anyhow.

The note had also arrived just after Yesenia had come back from a visit to StarReader HQ, one that had left her wan and gray and closeted in her office far too often.

Bean hadn't asked. Most of the secrecy that shrouded KarmaCorp didn't actually run all that deep—except for the layers that wrapped around Regalis Marsden and the tower where he sequestered the team of astrologers who watched over life, death, and everything in between.

The StarReaders made the skin between Bean's shoulder blades itch—but as Yesenia's right hand, she also had a clearer view than most on just how much of the good in the galaxy traced back to Regalis Marsden's tower.

Bean hadn't questioned the note. She'd come and cuddled a baby, and then another one, and now five years had passed and it had simply become part of her life.

She stepped over to the bassinet in the far back corner. Toby was one of the quietest nursery pod residents, and as a result, she had a theory that he got less attention. In a year or two she was going to have to teach him a bit about being a squeaky wheel, but in the meantime, she could make sure he got a little extra cuddling when she was around.

His eyes were awake and bright, watching the soft light show playing in the air in front of him. Bean toggled the switch to turn the lights off. "Hey, little guy. How about you come visit with me for a while and I tell you about my day, hmm?" She liked talking to the babies. They had such wise eyes.

Snuggling Toby in the crook of her arm, she headed toward the old gel rocker in the small room connected to the space where the littlest nursery residents slept. They could talk in there without disturbing any of the other sleepers. One of the very first things Bean had learned was just how irate the podcare staff could become if you woke a sleeping baby.

Something she understood far better after spending hours rocking one of them to sleep.

Toby wasn't going to be sleeping anytime soon, judging from the brightness of his eyes. She lowered into the squishy comfort of the gel rocker and settled the baby on her knees. His belly rumbled as he got situated, and she laughed. "Don't you go pooping on me now." The podcare staff were old school. No autodiapers, not on their turf. They went for the compostable ones, changed by human hands, and Bean had learned fast that podcare staff had a sixth sense about when to make themselves scarce.

Toby stopped his wiggling and she breathed a sigh of relief. "Thank you, sweetheart. It's been kind of a rough day." She really didn't need a stinky diaper to top it off.

Her captive audience blinked slowly.

She grinned at him. "Not as rough as yours, huh? Well, I had to deal with three lost apprentices, a shipping screw-up that sent all our new skinsuits to the Althusia sector, and an irate chef who can't figure out why he has to tolerate picky eaters in his cafeteria."

All while dealing with the quiet chaos of a boss who had vanished without a trace. Bean wasn't worried, exactly—not quite yet. Sometimes KarmaCorp had business sensitive enough that even the Director didn't know about it until she landed in it.

All Bean knew was that she'd received the quiet, coded message from StarReader HQ that meant Yesenia was away on official duties and nobody was supposed to get themselves twisted up in a knot—or ideally even comment on the fact that she was gone.

Bean snorted at Toby. "Like that's going to happen." Clearly, the StarReaders hadn't ever met a planet of inquisitive ten-year-olds and the bigger people they turned into. There was nothing the gossip channels of Stardust Prime liked better than a vacuum.

The Director had left her assistant a pretty mess to clean up. Bean sighed. Some things she couldn't say out loud, even if Toby's were probably the only ears awake enough to hear.

So she'd pick something that wasn't quite so classified to get off her chest. "I am kind of suspicious about those three trainees left on Vegas Station, I'll have you know. Shuttle captains aren't generally in the business of leaving passengers behind." Especially three very attractive teens who belonged to KarmaCorp. "What do you think the chances are that Trainee Mendoza has been practicing her hacking skills again?"

Toby blew some quiet spittle bubbles, as if considering just how easy it might be to delete three teenage names off a shuttle manifest.

Bean felt inclined to agree with him. "I could put Elsie Firenze on the job." The young Fixer was technologically adept enough to track whatever Addie Mendoza might have done, and enough of a troublemaker herself to put a good spin on it when she dumped the news into the Stardust Prime gossip chain.

And if the trainees had a small scandal to keep themselves occupied, perhaps they might not notice the Director was missing.

Bean raised her right eyebrow, tilted her head at wise-eyed Toby, and sighed.

If Yesenia wasn't back in twenty-four hours, her assistant was going to start raising quiet hell.

Even if she had to shake the leg of Regalis Marsden himself.

-ooo-

Yesenia stumbled out of the shuttle into the private docking bay on Stardust Prime, black dots swirling in front of her eyes. She was so terribly weak. The birth had drained her, but hiding the birth from the questing, seeking threads of time had exhausted her even more.

The threads had not understood that their exuberant joy was dangerous, that honoring the existence of new life put that new life and the entire fabric of the galaxy in deadly danger.

Or the fabric of the galaxy far in the future, anyhow. She had gone back in time as far as she could possibly reach. There were good reasons most Travelers went crazy. The human brain wasn't meant to dance across more than one timeline and make any sense of it.

Yesenia leaned against a wall, trying to hold herself up. After all she'd been through, she simply wouldn't permit her brain or her legs to give out on her. Not yet.

Not until she knew her daughter was safe.

Willing her legs to obedience, Yesenia pushed out with the last wisps of Talent she had left, reading the aura around the dirty, ill-wrapped bundle in her arms. Scanning, just as she had done relentlessly since the birth. Hoping she had enough Talent left to snip any threads trying to attach themselves. And felt the cell-deep relief at what she read.

She had succeeded. Followed Regalis Marsden's instructions to the letter.

She had found the lacuna in time where a pregnancy and birth might be hidden, clipped the threads, rewoven energy and history in a way no Traveler would ever attempt before or again. A relationship entirely unwoven from the knowledge of time. A baby with fuzzy red hair and golden eyes, rendered as unimportant as her mother could make her.

As far as the energies of the universe were concerned, this child was not hers.

Now she had to do the part that was going to kill her.

She had to keep it that way.

-ooo-

Bean felt herself startle to alertness, woken from a

very pleasant dream involving a sunny beach and a mindless novel, to stillness. To darkness. To the quiet comfort of the room that had been hers for eight years.

Back on Gastonia, waking up sharply had been a way of life. Here, she had gotten lazy. Complacent. Safe.

She strained her ears, trying to figure out what it was that had yanked her out of nocturnal bliss. A wandering trainee, perhaps, or someone's Talent gone a little astray? Several of the new class of tadpoles were abundantly Talented, and the youngest sometimes had trouble keeping things tamped down as they slept.

Even as she listened, she knew that wasn't what had called her out of sleep. Those kinds of disturbances were commonplace. She woke for those too, but gently, with the calm alert of a den mother who knew one of her charges was awake.

This was different. This had a knife edge, one that Gastonia's best greaser, lately retired, recognized all too well.

Whatever stalked in the dark, it carried danger with it.

It called on Bean to shield. To protect.

She swung out of bed, her feet brushing over the floor as she made her way in the dark to the small wardrobe. She contemplated a moment and ran her fingers over the neat line of hanging clothes. Normally she'd wander the halls in her colorful synth-silk robe and slippers, but this didn't feel like something she wanted to meet in her pajamas.

Going by feel, she pulled out the coveralls in

textured, tough fabric that had once been her standard uniform. Cheap, standard-issue protection worn throughout the galaxy. As a greaser, she'd put hers through harder duty than most. These days, it mostly served as gardening gear when she spent a day hanging out with the Lightbody clan. She dragged it on over her light sleepwear and felt better. As Yesenia's assistant, she generally saw it as her duty to wear things bright and flamboyant. It calmed those who needed a gentle distraction, amused those who knew her boss well, and disarmed a whole lot of people foolish enough to underestimate a woman in a colorful headscarf—or the woman who had hired her.

This night, she didn't want anyone or anything underestimating her.

Bean shoved her hands in her pockets and wished momentarily for the blaster that would have once ridden there. And then chided her own silliness.

She had never been that kind of warrior.

Grabbing a water tube and one of the apples that a trio of small Lightbodies had been handing out in the courtyard earlier, Bean slid out her door into the hallway.

Nothing stirred, not even the vague energies she'd learned to recognize as Talent taking an unauthorized nighttime stroll. But the knife edge hadn't gone away. Bean knew that was greaser sixth sense speaking, not Talent—but there were days when she thought maybe the two weren't all that far apart. Whatever it was, she'd always been smart enough to work with what she had.

She squared her shoulders and kept walking. If she

couldn't see what tried to touch her in the night, she darn well wanted it to see her.

Because she could feel the tug riding underneath the knife edge. The same tug that had pulled her here eight years ago.

For some reason—one that she might never understand—Lucinda Coffey was needed.

-ooo-

It was wrong, coming here like this, covered in cave dirt and whatever lived in the air of a century long past. But Yesenia knew if she waited a moment longer, she would never do what had to be done. She loved the child in her arms far too much.

Hopefully the dim of night would hide the dirt and the agony in her eyes.

She looked around the nursery pod where infants and young children slept, swathed in the slightly green glow of the floor-level lighting. Most parents on Stardust Prime opted for home supports once their babies were born, but a few preferred to hand their child raising off to the excellent staff hired for exactly that purpose.

She had never expected to be one of them.

Then again, despite the words of Regalis Marsden five rotations ago, she had truly never expected to be a parent. Thanks to her, the powers-that-be now knew that some implants didn't stand up well to trips through time. Sperm, however, made the voyage just fine.

An irony for another day—one when her heart wasn't threatening to break in two.

Yesenia looked down at the squashed face cuddled in her arms, knowing the child had her father's golden eyes. Asleep now.

Good. As foolish as it was, she didn't want her tiny girl to bear witness to her own abandonment.

She didn't want the energies of the universe bearing witness either. With fierce, unforgiving discipline, she pushed her feelings under. Away. Let the fog of exhausted stupor leach back into every corner of her soul.

A very tired Fixer wouldn't shake the vibrations in the galaxy overmuch.

A podcare assistant glided over almost soundlessly. "Hello, Director—may I help you?"

Yesenia turned to face the woman fully and kept her eyes on her child's sleeping face. "This is my daughter. I expect you to take good care of her."

The long silence spoke for itself. As did the matronly assistant's wide, astonished eyes.

It wasn't every day that someone disappeared out of time for three days and came back holding a baby. Yesenia knew better than to try to control the spin of that information. Gossip flowed fast and furious on Stardust Prime, and in this case, they were highly unlikely to guess the truth unless she willed it.

Instead, she would feed the flame of obfuscation. Anything to protect the child she must now release. "I know you weren't expecting her arrival. I also know you're fully staffed to handle an infant." She'd made it

her business to know, along with all the other prepara-
tions she'd laid in place since her terrible trip five years
ago to Regalis Marsden's tower.

Just in case.

"We are." The words were quiet, but managed to
convey a world of condemnation under the professional
non-judgment. "How long will she be staying with us?"

Some parents used the nursery pod for temporary
reasons. She could never be one of them. "She will
remain in your care." Yesenia could feel the anguish
trying to blast away her fog and stupor and ruthlessly
shoved it down. She held the child up toward the disap-
proving eyes and the kind hands. "Take her now."

The nurse reached out and briskly handled the trans-
fer. "You'll want a visiting schedule. Give me a moment
to get her settled, and I'll set that up for you."

She could never visit. They mustn't know she cared.
No one must ever know. She would not let herself be that
kind of threat to her child's safety. "I won't have time for
that. I have important work to do elsewhere."

Disapproval iced over into something far harsher.

Good. Her daughter would need all the protectors
she could get. She turned to go. She must not break.
Not here.

Not anywhere.

The threads of time must lie undisturbed. She had
done yeoman's work after the birth to steady them all.
She could not let a single moment of weakness shatter all
that work.

"Wait." The nurse somehow turned the single word

into a command, even as she crooned down at the now-awake baby in her arms. "What is her name?"

Yesenia managed a smile as her daughter waved a sleepy, disgruntled fist. "Her name is Tatiana." A bold and regal name for a child born under a scratchy blanket in a cave of dirt.

Her mother's one defiant blast at the universe.

Well, her second. Placing Tatiana here would be the other. It walked a very fine line with the instructions Regalis had issued. She would keep the child close so she could keep watch. Make it known she was Tatiana's mother for the protection that would bestow on her.

And suffer the agonies of watching her beautiful, bold girl grow up believing she had a mother who didn't care.

The universe must not know that Tatiana mattered.

Yesenia could feel the fog threatening to swallow. To overwhelm. To take what little life force she had left and transmute it into unending despair.

She must go now.

She could hear the nurse asking more questions as she left. She didn't stop walking. No one would question her—they would only judge, and she could live with that.

Her daughter was alive. Well and feisty and vibrant and safe.

And if her mother was very tough and very smart and very careful, this was only the first step in a long journey to make this right.

Because somewhere in the dirt of a long-ago cave, Yesenia Mayes had made a promise. One day, she *would* make this right. The energies of the universe did not get to take her daughter away. Not forever. That she simply could not bear.

She turned around and allowed herself one tiny moment of weakness. One last look at a head covered in red fuzz, and golden eyes that were sliding closed.

And then she stared down at the cave dirt on her empty hands and walked away.

-ooo-

Something wasn't quite right.

Bean tilted her head, eyeing what she could see through Yesenia's open office door at a slightly different angle. It had been bugging her all morning, that sense that something was missing.

Besides the obvious absence of the woman behind the shiny desk.

Bean picked up her third cup of coffee of the day, took a sip, and set it back down beside the tablet on her desk. She needed to get her mind on something more tangible than strange little niggles. She had work to do, and today it was going to require copious amounts of caffeine and actual focus to get the job done.

She'd walked the halls half the night, trying to find whatever had awakened her. It hadn't been until breakfast, when she'd walked into the massively stirred-up caf, that she'd actually found it—or the beginnings of it, anyhow.

Yesenia had arrived with a baby in the dead of night.

And then her boss had come to the office and generated enough messages and memos to keep the whole planet hopping for an entire rotation. Including one instructing Bean that Yesenia would be sequestered in her quarters until further notice, and attending to matters on her desk only at night.

Bean could only imagine the theories that would emerge once that pattern of behavior hit the airwaves. Yesenia Mayes, space vampire.

It told her assistant something quite different. Deep devotion to work, by someone who currently couldn't bear the light of day—and who couldn't sleep. The quiet, indisputable signs of someone in the grip of deep emotion or deep cracking. The sort of personal firestorm the Director would never expose to the public eye.

The kind she had left her assistant the quiet clues to see. After more than a decade of working together, they knew each other well enough for that.

Whatever had woken Bean in the night, part of what she was clearly supposed to protect was the vulnerable part of the boss lady's soul that most people didn't believe existed.

Bean sighed—that wasn't fair. People mostly believed what Yesenia wanted them to believe, and even then the smarter ones, who were legion on Stardust Prime, had their doubts. Which was currently driving gossip into a frenzy the likes of which had never been seen, at least not in Bean's time on the planet.

Scuttlebutt said that the Director had plucked some infant off a colony rock somewhere and decided to adopt her. The theories on how and why that might have happened were just getting more vivid as the day went on. Throw in the ideas of people who had remembered that Yesenia was a Traveler, and the level of crazy had ratcheted up to the point where Bean figured she could sell tickets and retire rich.

Except for the part where there actually was a baby. Bean had ducked into the zealously guarded nursery long enough to see the fuzzy red head and have a word with the tough and exceedingly kind woman who ran the place.

Tatiana would be very well cared for and protected exactly where she was.

Which left Bean sitting behind her desk trying to deal with everything else. She didn't even know where to start. Probably by getting straight in her own head.

That Yesenia had gone off on some wild assignment wasn't hard to buy at all. That she'd been gone nine months in some other timeline stretched the head a bit, but it was believable enough too. There was a reason the Traveler mystique existed, and a lot of it had to do with how much truth ran under the mythology.

But that Yesenia Mayes had claimed a child, or borne one of her own—and then handed her over to a podcare assistant?

Not a chance.

Bean knew why scuttlebutt was willing believe it—it fit all too well with the carefully nurtured persona of the stern, unyielding woman who ran KarmaCorp with a fiercely efficient hand and a polymer-coated heart.

It didn't, however, fit with the woman who sent Bean to check in on newly arrived tadpoles who might be crying in their sleep. Or the one who spent three days pacing her floor while galactic messengers tracked down a missing apprentice. Or the one who quietly put families of Fixers who went down in the line of duty on permanent KarmaCorp payroll, with jobs that met their real needs and bolstered whatever bits of hope and love they could still scrape together. It didn't fit with the woman who made sure the Seekers went into the dark alleyways and the gritty tunnels and the dusty colony streets looking for children with Talent—and feeding all the rest. In eleven years, Yesenia had doubled the number of trainees who weren't inner-planet born and done more for starving children than anyone in the quadrant.

In short, she was a fantastic boss, raising the finest crop of Fixers the galaxy had ever seen—and she did it in part by being a woman who deeply cared for the smallest, the weakest, and the most scared amongst them, even if she would have suffered the tortures of hell rather than admit it.

That was the woman Bean knew, the woman she'd worked alongside for eleven years and grown to cherish as a friend. And if that woman had left a baby in the arms of a podcare assistant, there was a deep and abiding reason for it. A reason Bean didn't even have the tiniest corner of, and that scared her silly.

Something was very badly wrong in the universe if Yesenia Mayes was abandoning her daughter.

Bean looked down at the handwritten note she'd

been crumpling half the morning. She'd dug it out of the depths of her personal filing drawer halfway through her first cup of coffee. The note that had asked her to show up in the podcare nursery five years ago.

Bean swallowed hard. Her boss would trust her to have a very long memory—and to understand what had never been said. Today she finally knew what the note had been asking of her. She might not know why, but in the end, that didn't matter.

Yesenia wanted her to watch out for a tiny, sweet girl with wispy red hair and golden eyes.

Because for some awful, universe-bending reason, her mother couldn't.

-ooo-

Yesenia slid into the nursery pod, moving on feet that were as silent as they were exhausted.

She'd spent the entire day in her quarters, meditating. Settling her mind. Resolutely pursuing equanimity, detachment, and sleep.

All she had achieved was new stiffness, new soreness to add to the old.

Her body was all too ready to remind her that she had recently given birth.

She clamped down sharply on the keening still burning in the center of her heart. Right now the biggest danger to Tatiana Mayes was her mother's weakness, and that simply wouldn't do. She could not allow herself to be the conduit of harm to her child.

Yesenia walked very slowly down the row of bassinets, noting the slow rocking of some, the quiet lights playing in others. Soothing, individualized to the needs of the current inhabitant.

She wished she could tell them that her daughter loved the stirring Russian songs of her great-grandmother.

The ones she must never sing again.

Yesenia's breathing stuttered.

She shouldn't have come. She was not strong enough to do this and keep her heart quiet. But if she didn't, the energies would see. They would sense what lived within her—and they would know.

Regalis Marsden had told her not to care. Not to love. Not to provide any kind of channel that would let the universe know how important Tatiana was, how important she could be.

Five years ago, Yesenia hadn't known to tell him that was entirely impossible.

But she was a Traveler, the most prodigious Talent that KarmaCorp had ever produced. If she could not stop loving her daughter, then she needed to build an impenetrable wall to hide the thing that simply refused to die.

With a strength born of exhaustion and torment and a love she never would have imagined possible, Yesenia Mayes stood in the nursery, ten steps from where her daughter lay sleeping, and pulled all that she felt into a tiny crevice inside her.

And then she shielded it with every magic and power and Talent she knew.

Only when that felt stable did she step forward again and close the final distance to Tatiana's bassinet.

She stood for a moment, feeling awkward and empty and bereft, clutching the worn rug in her hands. She stroked her fingers over the frayed edges as she listened to the whispered sounds of her daughter's breathing.

Knowing that she could not come again.

The fabric under her hands spoke of sturdiness. Of color and flamboyance and family and daring in the face of whatever life might bring. It held the energies of a place that knew of powers outside KarmaCorp's ken. It had been acquired in a moment that Yesenia hoped, with every cell of her being, connected to keeping her daughter safe.

Carefully, as if it were the most delicate spun glass, Yesenia laid the rug on the floor at the side of the bassinet.

It was only a rug—surely that wouldn't shift the threads of time overmuch.

NEXT IN THE SERIES, *Fortune's Dance*, which is Iggy's story. There's dancing. And cookies. And untangling the threads of the universe. (Which is good. Have a cookie. Raven wreaks havoc in this series after Iggy's book!)

Printed in Great Britain
by Amazon